THE
QUEEN'S
BLESSING

To our own Margaret of Scotland

THE UEEN'S LESSING

Madeleine Polland

ILLUSTRATED BY BETTY FRASER

HOLT, RINEHART AND WINSTON

NEW YORK · CHICAGO · SAN FRANCISCO

BOOKS BY MADELEINE POLLAND

The Queen's Blessing
The Town Across the Water
Beorn the Proud
Children of the Red King

FICM

ine!"

"No, mine!"

"Me! Me! Me!"

"Give it! Take your paws, you—!"

The pack of children swarming on the cobbled street screamed and cursed and jostled each other like the seagulls whirling over the cold gray, early morning sea. More of them came running with each moment, as if they were springing up out of the stones themselves, joining in the fight with teeth and nails and blue, bare feet; a seething mass of ragged hair and tattered, dirty clothes. Most of them had no idea what they were fighting over, only certain that where there was this noise and struggle there must be something at the heart of it worth the battle.

The something at the heart of it was one small fish, dropped from a laden creel as some successful fisherman walked from the wooden jetty to his home, or to the market with his catch, and over it the pack fought and bit and struggled until gradually the noise died down and a few of the smaller and weaker ones began to break away, shaking themselves after their battering, disappointment sharp on their small, pinched faces. The bigger ones fought on with no breath left for shrieking; only the silent struggle for even one raw, torn fragment of a small fish against the clawing misery of their hunger.

"Merca!" Suddenly one of the small ones yelled, a fair, soft-looking little boy who had left the fight quite quickly. He tried to rush in again to grab at his sister's skirt, his voice thin and high with fear. "Merca! I hear them! The Scots!"

It was not only his sister who heard him. To these hungry, homeless children, fighting for scraps in the burnt-out streets of Wearmouth in the year 1070, the word "Scot" was more terrible than homelessness and more frightening than starvation. The cry exploded the fight, and in one short instant they were all vanished and the narrow street leading down to the sea was empty, the cobbles greasy with the damp gray cold of February and the dull morning sky lying heavy above the burnt wreckage of small houses. The only sound was the dull thump and whisper made by the soft leather shoes of marching men who were not yet in sight, and the hard rattle of their arms.

As she leapt from the middle of the fight, the girl Merca grabbed the little boy who had shouted and whipped him along with her as she ran, plunging off the cobbled main street into the small, smelly side alleys where they slipped and slithered on the mud and refuse between the crowded huts of the fisherfolk, that alone remained standing in the ravaged town, too poor even for the attention of the Scots. They flopped down breathless in the end where the gray winter grass ran down a small slope to the sea's edge beyond the jetty, well clear of all the streets. There was no real need for them to hide; only to be sure that they were out of the way. The conquering Scots took little heed of children unless they found them directly in their path, and then a sword might come in as handy as a boot.

"I have it." Merca's grin was wolfish with triumph and

6

satisfaction. She pushed back the filthy, tangled hair from a face that had been pretty so short a time ago; round and soft and kittenish with the short nose and dark blue eyes of her Danish forebears. Only six weeks ago she had been safe, a stranger to hunger and loneliness and want in the homestead of her father, who was headman of his village and a good, prosperous farmer. Then King Malcolm the Third of Scotland had come down through Northumberland on his campaign of revenge, killing and burning and plundering across the fair farming land between Tyne and Tees in his mad anger against the allies who had forsaken him and Aedgar Aetheling as they struggled to defeat William of Normandy and put Aedgar back onto a Saxon throne for England.

The Danes who had promised to help him had fled the River Humber, their sails growing small and distant on the winter sea as they raced for their homeland. Gospatric of Northumberland himself had pledged help since Malcolm had sheltered him at an earlier date from William's anger, but he too had left them, turning south to make terms with the advancing Conqueror. Aedgar was now somewhere in the unfriendly wastes of the North Sea, aboard ship with his mother and his sisters, abandoned by the fleeing Danish fleet.

"And the best place, too," roared the thwarted Malcolm, "shut up in a ship with a pack of women. He should never have left his mother!" He put much of the blame for their failure on the weakness and stupidity of Aedgar, but being unable to reach him, he vented his anger on the hapless people in his path, raging through

Northumberland at the head of his army like a merciless torrent of destruction and death.

Merca and Dag missed their own death only by chance, being in the depths of the forest herding home the swine when the pillaging Scots had come swarming over the fields of their father's village. The army was already past when the two children came home through the dusk, to find a homestead where only trails of smoke rose straight and tremulous into the frosty air. Merca had taken Dag by the hand and started to run, and kept on running until they could run no more. Her only thought had been to get them both as far away as possible from the memory of what they had seen on that cold, beautiful evening, and at the end of weeks of hungry wandering with others like themselves, they had reached the small seaport town of Wearmouth. Malcolm and his men were there before them. The streets of the small town were already crawling with the homeless and the destitute, and half the houses were in blackened ruins, the ancient church of St. Peter lifting its burned out beams above them like a black skeleton against the pale skies of the turning year.

Merca already had stopped thinking about her home. A strange, hard darkness had come down between her and the memory of love and safety, and what it had been like to have enough to eat; the warm, gentle feeling of her mother's hands and the red fire of home in the evenings, with the mists of autumn striped across the fields outside. These things belonged to another world. Now she thought of nothing at all except avoiding the Scottish broadswords and finding enough food for her brother, with perhaps even a little for herself. She was only eleven and Dag was six, but already she had grown old, withered with cold and hunger and fear for both of them, for Dag, she thought, was simple, and could not live alone.

"I've got it, Dag," she said again, a little exasperated because he did not share her triumph.

"What?" asked Dag, who had already forgotten the fight over the fish, with the vague dreaminess that always left Merca to think for both of them.

"This, stupid one!" She unclenched a small blue hand, where the chilblains on all the knuckles had been scraped raw in the struggle, and showed him the crushed and mutilated fish tail, her eyes on his face, waiting for the cries of praise and pleasure.

Dag was unimpressed. He was as fair as she was dark, a blond, heavy, handsome child who lived somewhere in a calm, dreaming world all of his own, baffling Merca by never even seeming to notice their sufferings; taking everything that came to him but never troubling to find anything for himself, nor indeed complaining if he had to do without.

"You will die!" Sometimes she would scream at him, when she could rouse him to no effort, and he would neither beg nor steal nor try to fish. "You will die, die, die, and I won't stop you!"

He would smile at her then with his slow, sweet, loving smile and kiss her in silence as though to tell her that that was all he had to give; and loving him and hating him all in a tangle that she could not sort out, she would give him all she had and go hungry herself. Dag would never notice, his eyes vague and lost on the colors of the pale sea, and his fingers forever moving around the curves of a shell which he had picked up on the shore. Only at night time, when a dozen or more of them huddled together for warmth in some burnt, deserted homestead, did she know anything of what Dag felt. He was the one who wept most bitterly in sleep, calling and crying desperately for his mother. Merca held him to her tightly and fiercely and the hard darkness inside her grew steadily into a terrible burning hate of the Scots who had done this to him. In those cold nights, staring out over the huddled sleeping children to the starlit sea, she vowed to the God who seemed to have forgotten her that she would hate the Scots with every ounce of her growing strength until the day she died.

"I hate raw fish," the small boy said now, almost absently. "Can we not cook it?"

Merca looked at him in exasperation and then down at the small, squashed fragment of fish in her hands. Saliva gathered at the corners of her mouth and she felt as if her stomach was being squeezed in her efforts not to cram the miserable scrap into her own mouth.

"It isn't worth cooking, little brother," she managed to say gently. "Besides"—she took her mind for a moment off their immediate troubles—"I think we had better keep out of the way today. I don't know what it is, but there's something going on among these Scots. A fire might make them notice us. What do you think they are about?"

Dag turned and watched them too. The men who had

disturbed the fight in the street had now arrived down at the shore, a whole column of them, but they did not seem to be there for any particular purpose, standing idly beside the jetty, leaning in the loops of their spears and talking to each other. They were on the whole small men, but very broad with great quantities of thick black or sandy hair curling down over their foreheads, and with strong, sturdy legs. Dag turned away with a movement that was sharp for him, as though he was looking at something he could not bear. Then he shrugged and reached out an idle hand to take the fish, eating it almost absently. Merca turned away so that she did not have to watch him, but she couldn't fail to hear his teeth crunching on the bones, and she looked around desperately for something to distract her.

"Oh Dag," she cried. "Oh look—we hadn't noticed that!" She was truly distracted, jumping up to look along the river mouth toward the open sea. Dag got up, too, and turned his slow gray eyes in the direction she pointed.

"Isn't it a big one! We have never seen one like that before!"

Dag shook his head and swallowed, his eyes growing more alert. Merca was pointing at a ship that rode beyond the sandbars at the river mouth, and as Dag looked he felt the same happy feeling he had when he ran his fingers around his shell, sensing the soft run of its curving sides. All he could think about the ship was that every piece of her seemed to be in the right place, and she rode the sea as though she hardly touched it, her sail furled against a tall painted mast. He nodded with pleasure.

Merca was right. The ship was quite different from the rough, tubby fishing boats which were all they had seen before, and he liked her, but since he could find no words in which to say all this to his sister, he merely nodded again, watching the ship carefully, his own hands going up and down a little with her as she rode to the incoming tide.

"I wonder whose ship it is, and why it is here." Merca went on, always talking for them both. She shivered in the cold wind that was beginning to rise from the sea, blowing away the gray clouds of the early day to leave a sky of clear springtime blue, bright with cold. Her clothes had been poor enough before this morning's fight, her warm cloak long ago stolen by a bigger child. Now she struggled to hold together the tattered rags that let in every breath of the bitter wind. It rushed in from the North Sea, coming full over the flat land. Here the river mouth was fringed along its northern banks with the buildings of the ancient priory of Monkwearmouth, set between the sea and the level patchwork of good farming country.

The priory was behind the spot where the children had dropped onto the grass, and while Dag's eyes were fixed firmly on the riding ship, Merca had been watching sharply in all directions. She was not alarmed when she saw a small procession of four monks leave the priory through the wicket of the great gates, but she dug her brother in the ribs.

"They are making for the jetty, too," she said, "and we are much too close to it." She watched the four monks pass no distance from them, all black against the bright sky, their faces hidden by their hoods and their hands buried in their long sleeves. "The crowd grows big, my brother. Someone will notice us in the end." She was beginning to get anxious, looking around for some way they might escape without attracting attention from the crowd of soldiers at the jetty. Her thin face crumpled. It looked even more dangerous to go than to stay.

Dag took his attention from the ship, and gave it to his troubled sister.

"Get behind the boat," he said, wasting no words.

A little way from them an upturned skin boat was waiting to be recaulked, propped on two balks of timber that left a space beneath it. It was even closer to the jetty, but once underneath between the balks they would be well hidden, and one quick run would get them there. Merca looked at her vague little brother, and, not for the first time, thought that although he rarely spoke, when he did he was usually right.

"Clever Dag," she said, and he smiled at her amiably. "Are you ready to run?" He nodded, and together they bolted for the shelter of the boat, helped by the distraction of some fresh commotion at the jetty. No one heeded them, and they flung themselves into the close-smelling tarry darkness, crouching down so that they could still peer out and see what was going on. Dag saw with interest how the narrow space he peered through made all the colors of the day more sharp and clear. The grass looked greener and the winter sea more blue and bright. Merca was not looking at the colors of the sea.

"A-a-ah!" she said, and the fierce long-drawn hate of her cry made Dag turn to look at her, startled from his dreams. "A-a-h, it is him! What does he do here? And with such company, soldiers and monks to wait on him!"

From the cobbled main street out of which they had fled, a tall, heavy shouldered man had come striding into the crowd of soldiers on the jetty. He was accompanied by more soldiers, but it was impossible for the watching child to know if any were more important than the others. They all looked alike to her, except this one, who was different if for no other reason than that he stood half a head above the tallest of them all. His red hair flowed in heavy curls down to his shoulders and his beard jutted with the arrogant thrust of his chin. His shoulders were big and massive like an ox, and his great legs were muscular in their tight, cross-gartered trews.

"It is him," Merca said again. This time her voice was almost a whisper, hissing with her loathing of this man who had robbed her little brother of his childhood. She no longer gave any thought to what she had lost herself.

"The King?" Dag asked a little doubtfully, for he found it hard to sort these Scots one from another. He peered unwillingly through his narrow gap, preferring not to look at all. They all seemed the same, huge and hairy and threatening, filling him with terror and a strange sickening loneliness that he didn't understand, for he was already beginning to forget, when he was awake, that there had ever been any other life. He found it better not to think about the Scots at all. Merca would keep him safe.

"Yes, the King," she echoed him. "Malcolm, King of Scotia." Early on she had learned to know him as she and all the others like her peered from their hiding places to watch him pass. He had so easily overrun this little town, stripping the people and firing their church. Then, instead of passing on in his victorious sweep, he had stayed here, as if he waited for something, or someone.

There did not seem any great respect for him now among his men, who looked at him and stood about as they had stood before. He himself bent a hasty knee to one of the black-robed priests, who raised a hand in blessing, but before the gesture was half complete, Malcolm was already up again and gone.

Dag had been thinking.

"I think it is the ship, Merca. I think it is all to do with the ship out there."

He looked out at the ship again, framed in the small gap, her colors brighter now in the brightening day, and the sunlight striping the dark blue sea. He wondered what it would be like to be on board her, going up and down, up and down on those smooth waves. Merca grabbed him by the arm.

"Look, Dag. They are getting into a small boat to go out to the big one. You are quite right."

The party on the jetty were embarking in a rowboat, struggling down into it as it bobbed against the timbers, the disturbed seagulls screaming around their heads. One of the monks went first from the ladder, catching his foot in his long robes and almost falling, so that his hood fell back from his cold shaven head and the white fringe of

15

his hair. From above, Malcolm watched him and allowed him the courtesy of going first, but gave no hand to help him.

"See," hissed Merca. "See him, the proud Scot. He would not even give a hand to the holy Father, and he is old!" In the end it was one of the rowers who reached out from his place to steady the elderly priest, and then Malcolm himself leapt down, disdaining the steps and almost upsetting the boat as he landed with his great weight.

"Perhaps he is going away?" Dag suggested hopefully.

Merca shook her head.

"Why would he take a priest from here with him, and leave all these others waiting on the jetty? I think he is going to meet someone who has come on that ship. Our moth—someone once told me that when she was a girl she lived near a monks' house, and that the head monk always had to meet the important people who came to the village. I think that is why he takes the priest now."

The rowing boat and all the people in it now passed from their sight, around to the far side of the ship.

he morning by now was growing late, and the gentle February sun grew warmer, bringing a faint welcome heat to their chilly bodies. Gratefully Merca rolled over to where the warm light struck in under the edges of the boat, and turned her face up to the sun. It was the only comfort now that she ever knew, to find a corner of shelter when the sun was shining, and in the close protection of the boat she felt tired and drowsy and unwilling to move. With the soft heat on her face she was able, for a little while, to forget the ceaseless gnawing of hunger; able for a few moments to stop wondering what would happen if she and Dag could not find a home again or someone to look after them, or someone to feed them. Lately, in secret terror, she had begun to ask herself how long it took to die if you could not find enough to eat?

As the time passed, Dag grew restless in the small space.

"They are all gone, Merca. There is nothing more to see. Come on—let's go somewhere else." He was already halfway out of their shelter, and Merca turned on him in sudden fury, torn from her small moment of peace.

"And where?" she spat at him. "Where will we go? There is only one place for us, and that is out of the way of the soldiers! We are out of their way here, so there is no better place to go! Or perhaps you know where we can get our dinner!"

Dag stopped exactly where he was, on all fours half-way out from under the boat and turned to look at her. For one moment his face crumpled. Merca thought he was going to cry, and immediately her heart lurched with pity to see his round cheeks grown so thin and his gray eyes dark with the distress that she had given them. She reached out to comfort him, but Dag was stronger than she knew. He blinked a moment as if he shook him-self and then he moved at once back under the boat beside her, taking out his shell from his tattered breeches pocket. His fingers began to creep around its curves and he turned and smiled at his sister with his warm, steady smile.

"You are always right, Merca," he said. "Look, you are right about the king. He has gone to meet someone. How lucky we didn't go away."

He made his long speech slowly and then laid a cold dirty hand on her cheek and turned her face towards the sea. Obediently Merca looked, but for a while she could see nothing because she was blind with tears of helpless love for her strange, steadfast little Dag, and of hate and rage for all the Scots and the red-headed monster who was their king.

When the hot tears cleared and she could blink them from her lashes, she could not help but be interested. The boat was being rowed back from the ship, and now it was low down in the water that was bright with the strength-ening sun, green and pale above the sandbars and the shallows, and deep windy blue far out below the cold sky. Above the sea, the returning boat was a blaze of color.

Malcolm was dressed in hodden gray, and against this and the black habit of the monk, the cloaks of the new passengers glowed in green and blue and scarlet.

"Dag," cried Merca, all her troubles and anger for the moment drowned in curiosity. "It is three ladies!"

Dag watched for a long time in silence, and only as the company began to climb out of the boat up on to the jetty, did he answer her with one of his rare, deep chuckles.

"Looks like four ladies," he said.

First, three ladies had been helped up the narrow ladder, struggling with their colored skirts, but the fourth figure, in bright hose and scarlet cloak and long fair hair tumbling underneath a pointed cap, might easily have been a girl. He climbed gingerly up the jetty steps and minced along the broken timbers in distaste, frail and unlikely beside the broad and hefty Scots and dwarfed by the towering figure of Malcolm.

"I think he is young," Merca said, and she was smiling. She couldn't be sure about anybody's age but sensed some difference between Malcolm's heavy bulk and the thin figure that stepped beside him. "I wonder who they are?" Her smile faded suddenly to her more accustomed look of fear. "Oh, Dag! They are coming this way! They must be coming to the monks' house."

With rough gestures and a look of unwillingness, as if to make it clear that he had little time to spare for manners, the King of Scots had presented the more important of his followers to the three ladies, and, almost as an afterthought, to the young man in the scarlet cloak. This done, the whole company had turned and was moving along the path towards the priory across the fields. They were certain to pass within a few feet of where the children were hidden.

Merca felt her very fingers grow stiff with fear, and the hunger in her stomach was nothing to the crawling grip of terror. She had always been so careful that never before had they come as close to the Scots as this; and their monster king with them, and all his guests. She gathered enough of her wits to turn and pull Dag down and bid him keep absolutely silent. But there was no need for it. Dag was already crouched into the ground as if searching for protection like a little animal, his eyes wide and dark. Only his fingers moved, circling endlessly around his shell, quicker and quicker as the company drew near and fright closed in on him. Merca crouched beside him, helpless to protect him any more than at eleven years old, in a world full of enemies, she could protect herself.

Just as the bright whisper of the ladies' skirts, overborne by the rough rumble of Malcolm's deep voice, came close to them, Dag lost control of his terrified fingers. The shell shot out of them as wildly as if he had thrown it, and in stricken silence they watched it bumping down the small slope of short winter grass until it rolled to a standstill in the middle of the path, right in front of the advancing feet. It was more than Dag could bear. He had lost everything, and the shell was all he had for comfort. Fear of the Scots or of what he was about to do never entered his mind in the terror that his loved shell might be trampled underfoot, and before Merca could grab him, he wriggled out from under the boat and charged down to confront the advancing horde.

"My shell!" he shouted. "I want my shell!" Desperately he circled in front of them all, bringing them to a halt while he searched the ground, and then he looked up into the faces of the brightly clad women, far above him. "My shell," he screamed again. "My shell!"

Merca was beside him by the time the flabbergasted Malcolm found his breath and thundered out a burst of rage in which she understood only the command to kill them. Then, suddenly, before the men could move, the young woman who walked beside the King of Scots wheeled around and lifted a hand to stay them. She turned back and crouched down before the sobbing child, her wide blue skirts spread around her like a flower.

"I picked it up," she said. "I picked it up for you." She spoke strangely and Merca had difficulty in understanding her, but her voice was slow and gentle and filled with a sweetness that both children had forgotten. For a long moment, everyone was silent, watching her, and the small boy stared close and astonished into the fair young face as if he had seen an angel, the tears still trickling in a pathway down his dirty cheeks and his hand reaching out to take the precious shell. In the freshening wind the girl's blue hood had blown back from her lovely face, showing it framed in red-gold hair, and Dag's eyes rested on it once his shell was safe, thinking that it looked like the tall gray trees in some place he had once lived, when all their leaves turned to this color before the winter came. She smiled from one child to the other, and her gentle face was full of pity as she laid a finger on the thin bones of Merca's cheek and then rose quickly, turning to Malcolm to pour out a flood of pleading which the children could not understand.

During this time the other young woman had shown nothing but impatience, tapping her foot on the ground and tossing her dark head, and as she listened to what her sister said to the king, she clucked with scorn and set off alone along the pathway, followed by the anxious prior. Nor would Malcolm listen to the fair one, although he did not treat her with the brusque rudeness which he kept for other people. Over and over again he shook his head, and the lovely girl went on begging, until, in the end, with a gentleness that seemed strange and foreign to him, he took her by the arm and turned to the older woman, asking her to go on to the priory. He himself led the fair one, unwilling and protesting. He turned only to fling one last order at the men as he went.

The girl looked back at the two children as she was led away, and now it was her cheeks that were wet with tears as the rough Scots' hands seized the boy and girl and began to pull them away. Merca barely felt it when the soldiers pulled her away, for capture was something so long feared that it meant little now that it had actually come. Her mind was full of the strange lady, so beautiful and so gentle and so kind.

"Where are you taking us?" she asked at last, as they were hustled back towards the town. "To kill us?" Even that did not seem real or possible in the same moment as she remembered that calm and lovely face. Nor was

it real to Dag, for he had got back his shell, and even though the Scots had got him at last, it did not seem so terrible now that it had happened. They were all laughing and talking amongst themselves, and Merca was with him, so everything was going to be all right. His thumb smoothed the gentle surface of his shell and he thought with pleasure of the soft face of the lady who had picked it up.

The soldier answered in a rough Saxon, his words twisted into the odd shapes of a man who was more used to the quick race of Gaelic.

"You are the lucky ones," he said, not unkindly. "For King Malcolm said not to kill you, to please the lady."

Now Merca really looked at him. Scots soldiers did not usually think much about killing, and the king was well out of sight.

"What then? Where are you taking us?" She held tightly to Dag's hand.

Above the tangled dark red beard, the freckled face split into a broad grin, and pleasure gleamed in his crinkled eyes.

"To Scotia, girl, to Scotia! Where else? The King's away for home now, and we with him, and there's a good bag of money to be gathered on the march home for all the slaves we can take!"

"We are to be sold as slaves?" In the bitter wind, she did not think it possible for her to grow colder, but she felt fear like an icy band around her forehead.

"Not Dag," she cried then. "Not Dag! He is too young to be a slave."

Dag lifted an anxious face. "What is a slave?"

Merca knew. She had listened to too much talk among the homeless children.

"It is nothing, Dag. He is too young!" she cried again to the soldier.

The man looked down at her. Nothing could disturb his good humor today, now that he knew that he was going home.

"That is Dag?" he asked, giving the boy a push with the butt end of his spear that sent him stumbling along the street, and guffawing at the name. "Dag is big enough," he said, giving him another push that sent him sprawling. "Big enough! And he will grow!"

Merca pulled the little boy to his feet, and they looked at each other as they were marched past the jetty. There was nothing to say, and nothing they could do. Dag did not understand the future, only that the Scots had got him at last. Merca understood a little, and stared hopelessly at Dag and he stared back at her. Could it be any worse than what had already happened? Only, only, thought Merca grimly, they must stay together, for without her Dag would die. She tightened her grip on his cold fingers. He was no use by himself. Alone he would die.

In a while she thought again of the strange lady who had come ashore from the ship. She and Dag were by now part of a crowd of starving scarecrows like themselves, children and grown-up people too, who had been rounded up from their hiding places where they thought they had been safe. The Scots knew exactly where to look, simply having left them there in their foolishness until the day came that they would march them north and sell them. Now they had been herded together in the small square in the middle of the town, some of them weeping silently and hopelessly, and some of them screaming and protesting, only to be silenced by the soldiers with the flat of their swords. Most of them though stood like Merca and Dag, quite still and silent, hand in hand, looking into a shapeless future that could surely be no worse than the past. Merca had at least got something to remember. The same soldier was standing close beside them, and she turned to him.

"Who was she?" she asked him. "That lady?"

The soldier was still in high good humor and was prepared to waste a moment to answer.

"The lady?" he said importantly. "You mean the princess?" Merca struggled to follow him, understanding him to say that the lady herself was the Princess Margaret, and the other two her mother and sister, the Princesses Agatha and Christina. They were kin to the Confessor who ruled England before Norman William took it by the sword. Now, it seemed, King Malcolm had been fighting to win England for the Princess Margaret's brother Aedgar, the young man in the scarlet cloak, and here the soldier snorted in disgust, saying that Malcolm had had little success for all those who had promised to help him and young Aedgar had fled. So today, Aedgar and his mother and sisters had arranged to seek shelter at the court of King Malcolm, and now Malcolm was away home with his army, to be ready and waiting to welcome the family when they should reach Scotland by sea.

Merca did not really follow him, nor understand, nor care. She had never known who ruled England. She had only known the small, safe kingdom of her own home; a world of warmth and happiness where every tomorrow had been as certain as today. Now it had all vanished, and there was nothing at all but the small, cold hand of Dag within her own and the hunger in her stomach and a future that was all darkness. The face she had seen today hung in her mind like a lamp against her loneliness, and out of the soldier's story the only thing she picked was a name.

"Margaret," she said to herself quietly. "Margaret." It gave her the same comfort as Dag found in fingering his shell.

erca and Dag were almost the last ones of their band to be disposed of. In all the market places through which they passed, in the small gray towns, and among the huddled wind-swept buildings of bleak farms and country houses, the soldiers offered what they had for sale. The children grew accustomed to the brightening eyes that roamed over them, like those of a thrifty housewife who is faced suddenly with a bargain she did not expect. One by one they saw the others go, trailing away hopelessly in the footsteps of their purchasers, and Merca clung grimly to Dag's hand and watched in terror as she saw families split apart and children separated, driven off in different directions with as little thought as if they had been new-bought cattle. They were silent now, most of them, and hardly objected; too cold and hungry and desperate after the long, starving march to raise the energy for tears. Dag pressed close beside her as the number left grew smaller and smaller; only the sick remained now, the poor bags of bones that no one wanted and a few of the children, too frail to be thought much use.

"They will not make you and me go to different places?" Dag asked her, fearfully. He was not as simple now as he had been, and had no longer any doubts as to what it meant to be a slave, nor had he still his blind faith that Merca could protect him from everything. His sister's fingers were so tight about his hand that he looked at her, wondering why she hurt him.

"Never, never, never," she said through her teeth. "We will always be together, no matter what comes."

In her mind, she and Dag were one, and she answered him so fiercely that she almost convinced herself that she could keep it so, but with every homestead that came into view along the frozen ruts of the road, and every town that lifted its roofs above the fields, she was sick with terror lest someone would say, "I will have the girl, but not the young one." What could she do then against the soldiers who were growing tired of trailing these last, slow-moving ones along, anxious to get going faster on the road and also to get some return for the odd lumps of porridge and the occasional bowls of soup that they had laid out to keep them alive.

There was little discipline in the way in which Malcolm's fighting men returned home, trailing in disordered groups with their bunches of captives and their pack horses and their own backs laden with bundles of booty from the ransacked homesteads of Northumbria; struggling along the desolate roads in the Scottish winter— for up here it was still far from the thought of spring, with snow drifting in the freezing winds across the barren hillsides and ice to be broken on the small streams where they looked for water. The two children had forgotten that there ever was a world of warmth and food, as they crouched with their lumps of porridge at a distance from the soldiers' fires and clung together through the bitter nights for what warmth they could get from each other. Now they did not speak much, nor did they look any longer like children, living and moving in silence as if they had grown old, too weary to be troubled with talking. Only in their clinging hands did they show the bond between them, and it was in silence, hand in hand, that at last they faced the woman who was going to own them.

She was waiting on the side of the windy, snow-swept road, word having gone ahead of the soldiers that there was cheap labor to be had in the way of captives from the English raiding, and long before they came up to her her sharp eyes were raking the few sorry remnants that still trailed along. In the last few days many had been left beside the road without even the mercy of a clean sword cut.

"I've little to give you," she said sharply to the soldiers the moment they came abreast of her. Merca watched her face anxiously, not understanding. She was almost as thin as the children themselves, but rawboned and skinny with hard work and mean living, not from starvation. From above her high red-veined cheekbones, her sharp eyes looked appraisingly up and down the collection of poor scarecrows.

"If that's the case then, mistress, it's little you'll get." One of the men answered her as sharply as she had spoken, and she sniffed.

"It's little you have to offer," she countered, and the man was silent, knowing it to be true. Her face was as gray and bleak as her hodden dress and the coarse cloth wrapped around her hair, and it seemed to Merca that she was just another part of the dead, snowdrifted landscape that climbed to the gray sky behind her head.

30

"A child would do me," she said and although Merca still did not understand the Gaelic words, a fear as hot as fire shot through her frozen body and she gripped Dag's hand and tried to ease herself away as if she hoped to make them both invisible. She knew with sick certainty that the cold hard eyes were resting on her as the woman spoke even though she did not understand the words. On her and not on Dag.

They burst then into bargaining, the soldiers obviously refusing what she offered and bargaining with her in return. Unable to follow, Merca turned frantically from face to speaking face as the wind whipped along the bare upland road, blinding them all with fine snow, and she could see that the men were giving in, anxious to be on their way out of the cold and the discomfort. Terror took her by the throat.

"I will not go without Dag," she screamed. She was afraid of nothing except leaving him, for he would die. "I will not go without Dag!"

They all turned and looked at her in astonishment, as if they bargained above the dumb head of a sheep and it had turned and spoken. There was a moment of absolute silence, filled only by the whining of the wind across the bare land as they were struck by a fresh flurry of snow, and above them the gray sky was weighted with the burden of more to come. It seemed to be the weather in the end that made the men make up their minds, driven to some conclusion by the icy wind. They spoke together a moment and then one of them turned to the woman, and Merca, unable to breathe with fear, saw her look in obvious surprise at Dag, unable to resist a bargain. His blond good looks were gone, his legs now as thin as sticks and his thick hair dead and brittle round his pinched face, but he was still a big boy for his age and she could not bring herself to turn him down.

In the end they saw her nod, but did not dare to turn their heads to look at each other, for even the dreamy Dag had known that he was on the edge of being torn away from Merca, and while he had neither screamed nor spoken, his fingers, deep in his ragged pocket, had been whirling frantically round his shell. Gradually they slowed, as still fearful but growing more sure, he stood with his hand in his sister's and watched the small tally changing hands between the woman and the soldiers. They trudged off along the road with the last few of their captives who dropped their hopeless heads to the bitter wind; and the children themselves felt it pierce to their skin under their miserable rags as they stood there on the frozen ruts, waiting for their new life to begin.

It began almost at once as the woman struck Merca a blow on the side of the head that sent her sprawling, her hand wrenched from Dag's.

"Get you on," she cried in Gaelic, but the gesture was unmistakable. "Think you I paid for you to stand there idle!" And you too, boy! Don't think because I only paid for one of you, that the two won't have to work! And what's more, there will only be food for one."

So there was food only for one through all that remained of that bitter winter, when they struggled from sleep in the cold scarlet dawns, leaving the smelly straw that was their bed on an outhouse floor for the long day of labor that would not end for them till darkness. Merca worked in the house and the dairy, and Dag, far beyond the limits of his strength, toiled about the farm that had no labor for its acres except the silent and spiritless husband of the woman who had bought them. They were driven from task to task with a kick and a curse and a blow for every thing in which they failed, and quite often for nothing at all, and their stomachs were continually torn with hunger, for the woman was true to her word and there was never enough to eat.

"I am still hungry," Dag would whisper to Merca at the beginning, but after a while he grew silent, knowing that she had nothing she could spare. As time passed, they did not notice the hard work so much, for they grew used to the fact that every bone ached with endless weariness. But they never grew used to their hunger, and they had not been long in the house before the woman came to understand the fear that lived with Merca.

"I will send the boy away," she would threaten her for every little fault, overshadowing each day with terror and uncertainty, watching the girl with bright, malicious eyes as she spoke, and enjoying her anxiety.

Day followed day, every one the same endless burden of work as the last, and the brother and sister barely noticed the changing seasons of the year. They took no heed of the green tide of spring creeping like a stain over the barren upland fields, or the yellow haze that misted the black skeletons of the winter trees. They knew the summer only for the fact that they were warm when they slept at night, the day's work was longer and harder, and Dag was exhausted by the work in the fields in the hot sun. He was growing fast on half enough to eat.

They never even saw the sweet colors of the summer, or heard the larks shrilling to the soft skies, or lay idle among the flowers along the stream to watch the minnows darting in the shallows. They had forgotten that they were children or had any right to the summer pleasures they had once known. One day, Merca took the husband's dinner down to the far fields where Dag was working with him, and the man looked at their faces as he unwrapped the hot savory pie and he moved as if to give it to them, and then glanced in fear at the distant house and set it aside. He laid a hand on both their heads and looked at them, shaking his own sadly, but they did not know what he meant. They had forgotten kindness, nor did he dare persist, but snatched back his hands with another fearful glance toward the house and ordered them to work.

The short summer drifted into the red-gold days of autumn when the sweep of distant hills was hazed with the soft colors of the heather and the berries on the windswept trees hung red as the frosty skies at dawn. As the days shortened and the deadening mists crept over the lonely country, autumn darkened again into cold winter and the two children still lived without hope. They thought of nothing beyond struggling through each day, and of whether there would be even half enough to eat at the end of it before they huddled in silence onto their dirty heap of straw.

Dag's eyes were no longer dreaming. They had grown empty and vacant, resting on nothing, and he rarely spoke, nor did he any longer smooth the curves of his shell, although he kept it carefully knotted into the corner of his shirt as the pockets of his outgrown breeches had long since worn away. Now and again he took it out and looked at it, and turned it over and over in his fingers as if it reminded him of something, and puzzled him. He would look at Merca as if he was about to ask her something, but he always stopped and put the shell away, saying nothing.

His sister watched him, but even she no longer had strength to care. Dag's plight tore at her less fiercely because she was struggling so desperately with her own, and so they drifted into the deep days of their second winter, no longer children, no longer feeling much about anything at all, grown through hunger and neglect to be a little less than human.

Merca woke suddenly one night, starting up from the dirty straw beside Dag, unable to think what had wakened her. She sat and stared round the familiar shadows of the wattle outhouse where they slept, seeing the familiar shape of shafts rearing to the roof, and of ploughshare and baled hay. She heard from the stable next door the soft, restless movements of the horse and she was not frightened. It was not fear that had roused her, nor a dream, nor was she unusually cold. They were used to cold now, and it had to be very bitter to disturb their exhausted sleep. Tonight the air beyond the open end of the thatched barn was mild and soft, and the patch of sky which she could see was ablaze with stars against a milky darkness. Then in the silence, she heard once more the sound which had disturbed her, although it was far and faint, blown in gusts on the night wind; the clear, sweet sound of distant bells.

Alert as she had not been for many months, she knelt up in the straw beside her sleeping brother and strained her ears toward the sound. All at once the faint, falling chimes and the stars that blazed in the dark night whirled together in her mind to form a memory, long faded, of her father harnessing the old bay horse to the farm wagon on just such a night as this of starlit, windy darkness, and strange, excited expectation. They had driven, warm-wrapped against the cold, across the hills to some vast building where the air was filled above their heads with the roaring clangor of such bells. Then there was silence and a blaze of golden light and the voices of men singing; and a feeling that the whole world was rejoicing. At home afterward, there had been food and laughter and a great hot fire, with a baby lying beside it in a basket.

She stared at the stars beyond the shed, and her numbed mind struggled with the memory.

"Dag!" she cried suddenly, and turning around she beat him furiously on the back with her fists. "Oh, Dag, Dag! Wake up! It's the Feast of Christmas!" Her starved face was radiant with happiness, full of excitement, the present completely forgotten in the warm certain delight of the past.

Dag roused slowly.

"What?" he said. "What's the matter?" He was awake

but uninterested, dully expecting nothing but more trouble of some kind, and unwilling to face it.

"Dag!" she cried again, and took him by the arms, while he stared with stupid amazement at the bright happiness of her face, clear in the soft starlight. "Oh, Dag, it's the Feast of Christmas!"

He looked at her with his dull eyes for a long time, and then he shook his head.

"What's Christmas?" he asked, but he did not really care.

Nothing in all their desperate plight had so upset her.

"You remember! You *must* remember Christmas! We took you, even though you were so small!"

Hopefully, she jogged at him with all the details she could remember, trying to light a spark of memory or interest in his thin, dull face. But Dag shook his head and did not care, sinking lower and lower onto his straw, his mind only on the speed with which dawn would come and he would have to wake again.

"You *must* remember!" For some reason, nothing in the world had ever seemed so important to Merca, and she struggled to recall all she had been told of what the Feast meant. For the first time since she had run from home, she allowed her mind to grasp the memory of her mother's voice, and she began telling Dag urgently about the baby in the stable. Looking around at the wattle shed where they were themselves, she said, "Rather like this, Dag, I should think. They must have been rather like us."

She told him as best she could about the three wise men, and looked out again at the stars and remembered the piece about the angels singing above the heads of the astonished shepherds.

"Oh, Dag, surely you remember?"

Dag was sound asleep, sprawled on the straw with his eyes closed, indifferent to the starlight.

She did not cry. She sat and listened to the silence that followed on the bells, and it was as if some part of her that had grown still and dead during these last months came slowly to life again. Life had been so hard that she had forgotten to fight for Dag, who could not fight for himself; she had just been living for every day and putting up with things. She had even forgotten to hate; forgotten what she felt about the Scots who had so destroyed her little brother. Now all her hate and bitterness came rushing back, filling her small body like a storm, so that she laid her head down on her knees to try and bear it. She had borne a lot, but for some reason that she did not understand, it was beyond all things that she could bear that Dag could not remember Christmas.

Hatred and the will to fight hardened in her again, and she looked out once more at the stars that blazed down over the now silent world. The Scots should not have Dag, and she would hate them till the day she died.

"It will be stupid now," she said aloud, and Dag did not stir. "But as soon as the year turns, we will run away. We will find somewhere to live for ourselves. I will look after him."

ag, have you any idea where the north is?"

Merca pushed aside the bushes at the edge of the wood, and looked out around the ring of sky above the soft spring country, sighing heavily to find that it all looked exactly the same to her. Surely there should be something different about the north, or else how did people know where to find it? She turned back to Dag, who did not seem to have heard her, and asked the question again.

"What is the north?" Dag said then, nor did he care about the answer, and Merca could have shaken him. The flame of determination kindled in her by the Christmas bells had never wavered, and true to her resolve, at the first burst of warm weather, they had run away. She was filled with irritation, however, that she could not raise Dag's enthusiasm to the same pitch as her own.

Her chance had shown itself on the previous evening when the sun had set in a drifting haze of rosy pink that told them—country children—of fine days to come; and the whole moist, shadowed evening was soft and rich with the promise of spring. She had been watching for just such an evening, growing edgy and impatient as the cold winter of the north dragged on and on into the year. It did not seem to occur to the woman who owned them that they would have the strength or courage to escape, and they were never shut in in any way. No one would miss them until morning.

"Now," she said urgently to Dag, her thin face taut with her determination. "Now! We will go this evening as soon as it is dark. We will never get a better one." They had no preparations to make, having nothing they owned and no one to leave behind.

Dag was strangely unwilling, as though he had rooted himself in this wretched life, and was afraid to change it lest the next thing might only be worse. Merca snarled with irritation, keyed up through long weeks of resolve, and then in the fading light she caught the look of dead weariness in his eyes. Her voice grew more gentle but her resolve hardened. Dag was too tired to care, but that did not matter, for she could care for both of them, and somehow they would find a better way to live.

"Nothing can be worse than this, little brother!" She knelt beside him in the straw and the whole shed was filled with the last rosy light of the sunset, while in the trees outside a blackbird piped his pleasure in the spring, sweet and true and bright with promise. "There can be nothing worse than here. We'll find some way to live. Please, Dag!"

Dag gave way because he had not the energy to do anything else, and as soon as the last light faded from the sky and the blackbird had fallen silent, they set out hand in hand across the dark fields. Cautiously they glanced back at the rough timber house with its fringe of tattered thatch, but there was nothing there to fear. No light gleamed from the one window, for the woman was too mean even to waste a saucerful of tallow, and she and her meek husband retired to bed, like the children, at the fall of dusk. From the end of his chain ringed into the stable wall, the farm dog fawned and stretched at them and whined a little, but raised no noise, for he was used to their movements close beside him at night. Almost too easily they struck across the fields with the grass wet about their ankles and the damp smell of the soil rising in the night, soon setting considerable distance between them and the farm.

"Where are we going?" Dag asked after a while. He had not spoken since they set out, plodding in silence after Merca, who kept up a faint whispered chatter to encourage him, to which he answered nothing. She was delighted to be able to tell him something, hoping to kindle in him some life and interest in the adventure that would make it easier for him.

"You know the long field where the barley grows, and the small stream runs across at the bottom?"

In the darkness, she felt rather than saw Dag nod his head.

"Well, if you stand at the top end of that field, you can see in the distance a long line of forest. I make for there. It should not be too hard, because you can look straight across to it, and if we reach it in darkness it will be somewhere to hide when morning comes. They would catch us too easily if we were still in the fields."

The idea of being chased seemed to strike the small boy suddenly.

"Will they come after us?" His voice was touched with fear.

Merca did not know what to say, wondering if it would

frighten him too much if she were to say "yes," or if it would stir him to move a little faster. The darkness was lit now by a blunted moon riding the high clouds, and by its light she peered at him for a clear moment and met the sharp question in his eyes.

"Yes, Dag," she said. "When it is day and we are missed, then I am sure they will come after us. Do you think our good Mistress would waste the money she paid for us?"

In the fitful light she sensed the faint glimmer of a smile from Dag, the first for many months, and his feet quickened their pace beside hers. They were both a little more alive for being free and on the move, but Merca waited in fear that he was going to ask her where they were making for, and this she could not answer him, because she knew no more than he did. She had a faint idea of finding the place where the bells had sounded, for where there were bells there must be monks, and in the little ravaged town of Wearmouth, the only people who had ever managed to spare a bite of food or a bowl of soup for the starving had been the monks. But the bells had pealed faintly out of an empty sky, and she had not the slightest idea which way to turn to find them.

They reached the belt of woodland in the deep, silent, creeping dark that comes before the dawn and before the first bird sings, and Merca closed her fingers tight on Dag's in front of the black, formless wall of the trees. Firmly she told herself how much more dangerous it would be to be out in the open when daylight came, and although she trembled from head to foot and her heart felt strangely as if it had slipped into the middle of her throat, she marched blindly and determinedly into the darkness of the woods, with Dag stumbling behind her.

They could see nothing at all, and hear nothing but the brush and scuff of their own uncertain footsteps and the quick, vanishing rustlings in the bushes as small creatures fled out of their way. Branches of the undergrowth reached out to brush suddenly at their faces and tangle in their hair, and now and again they tripped over some roughness on the ground, but they were by now too frightened even to cry out when they were taken by surprise. At last they could no longer see the faint shadowed edge of the trees; only blackness whichever way they looked. After several tries, Merca found her voice.

"We should be safe here until it grows light and we can see." She tried to steady the quavering. "Sit down, Dag," she managed more firmly. "Sit down and rest."

Cautiously they eased themselves onto the ground, feeling the dampness of dead leaves and moss and the sharp prickle of a broken branch, and they leaned on each other in the silent darkness with watching eyes strained wide. Suddenly, the first awakening bird began to cheep and in a few minutes the whole wood grew wild with bird song. With long breaths of relief they saw the tops of the trees begin to show clear against the brightening sky, and looked at each other with shamefaced grins as the first gray daylight strengthened through the green of the empty woodland.

Now they crept to the edge of the open land to try and decide what they should do next. For some time after dawn Dag had slept, but Merca had not dared, for she did not feel them far enough from the farm for safety, and she watched and listened anxiously for any sounds of pursuit. She herself would have gone on, under cover of the forest, but Dag was too tired.

"Where is the north?" she said again, almost to herself.

On the march before they were sold, the soldiers were always talking about the north as the direction in which they must go, and they had been making for Scotia, since that was their home. Carefully, she had worked out that if she could find her way back along the same route, the opposite way to the north, then that must lead back toward her own home, or where her own home had been. In the first shock and fright at the sight of her burning home and dead parents, she had taken Dag and run and run, as far and as fast as she could. But now in her determination to find a new home for Dag, she had been remembering that there had been friends and neighbors close by who might look after them if only they could find their way back there.

And now Dag answered by asking where the north was, and she grew irritable.

"Oh, Dag, the north! The north—it's where—it's . . ." She fell silent, despairing, for how could she tell Dag what the north was when she did not know properly herself; just that it was some place where Scotia lay, so home must be the other way. A country child, she knew in which direction it lay by the sun, but the day was dim and clouded and in the thick wood she had not thought to look for the direction from which the first light had come. It was all too much to explain to Dag, and she peered out in silence from the bushes that hid them. They had crossed the belt of forest, though in what direction Merca did not know, and now they were on the other side, facing a long stretch of rough, hilly country that seemed empty of any life at all except for a few sheep scattered in the distance, bent to the wiry grass.

"I think we could go on from here in daylight. It looks so empty. What think you, Dag?" She tried again to interest him, but although he did not answer, this time his eyes were far from empty. They were large and black with fear and he crouched stiff against a tree trunk.

"Listen," he whispered. "Listen."

Merca listened, and knew she should have heard the sound before if her thoughts had not been so full of going on. Behind them through the wood came the short familiar barking of a dog.

"It is them," Dag whispered again. "After us. It is the dog." In the unfriendly household, the poor animal had never known a name, and the only friendliness had come from the two children, who looked on him as a captive like themselves, and spoke to him when they could and treated him with kindness.

Frantically Merca glanced around for shelter, her eyes as wide and panic-stricken as the little boy's, but it was the slow and silent Dag who spoke first.

"The hole," he said, on a gasping frightened breath, but Merca knew at once what he meant. Not a stone's throw back, as they made their way through the wood, Dag had almost vanished, floundering suddenly up to his waist in a depression in the ground that was filled with dead leaves. Merca had pulled him out, and they had gone on their way. Now without another word, they scrambled from under their bushes and rushed back until they found the spot, digging themselves in frantically under the rotting leaves and the soft crumbling mold as the sound of voices grew clearer through the trees, with the occasional bark of the dog and the crack and rustle of trampled undergrowth.

They were barely below the surface of the leaves, scrabbled so desperately over them, but the cold, dank smell was suffocating. Merca groped for Dag's hand as the scuffling in the undergrowth grew close, and the eager panting of the dog seemed almost on their heads. She pressed her face tight into the mold and almost ceased to breathe, knowing that their life as it had been before would be a paradise compared to what it would be if they were captured and taken back. Beside her, she could hear Dag sobbing quietly and despairingly, and she squeezed his fingers tight and listened to the short, sharp barks and eager whines with which the excited dog told of what he had discovered. He knew it was the children who were kind to him, and he was delighted to have found them. Eagerly he began to dig.

They heard footsteps rushing up to him, and then, incredibly, the voice of the husband bidding him urgently to hold his peace. Time had taught them to understand the Gaelic, and amazed they listened to the argument between the man and the dog; the dog determined to unearth what he had found, and the man determined to shut him up. The dog yelped suddenly as if he had been struck and then grew silent and they heard the man's footsteps move away, followed by a reluctant slithering as if he dragged the dog.

In a few moments, his voice called out.

"There is nothing here, do not trouble to come! I have been to the edge of the wood and there is nothing! We will try the other side—they could not have got further this way."

"I thought I heard the dog." The woman's voice answered, and they could hear the eager crashing of her feet.

"A coney," the man called back. "A coney! It got away!"

For a long time after the last sounds had died away, they lay still where they were, unable to believe it true, but then at last they sat up and stared at each other, and Merca leaned over to pick off the dead leaves where they clung to the tears still wet on Dag's cheeks. For the first time in many long months, they smiled broadly, like the children they were. This time they could not miss it. They had met kindness again and knew it for what it was. It filled them both with high spirits and new determination, even though their empty stomachs now gnawed at them like rats.

Through the long hours they walked on the ridges of rough hills, strong with their new sense of purpose, so that Merca was hardly troubled when Dag at last said:

"Where are we going to, sister?" He was complete in his confidence that she would know.

"We are going to the south," she told him firmly, having

during the day remembered that the south was opposite to the north, so to the south they must go. She did not tell his contentedly nodding head that she still had no idea where the north was, however hard she scanned the clouded sky. For the moment anyway, she was more concerned about finding food for them, or they would be worse off even than before.

The little boy was quite satisfied.

"What will we find there?" he asked, and his sister's face darkened.

"No Scots, at any rate, and no vile King of Scotia. Only our own people, who should look after us."

They tramped over high ground through what seemed to be an empty world beneath a milky sky, soft with the even light of the hidden sun. They came across only one lonely farmhouse with its brown thatch so melted into the folds of the hills that they were on it unexpectedly and Merca was filled with panic and the fear that barking dogs might bring a household running to the noise.

"Quick, oh , quick!" she cried to Dag, and ran him back the way they had come until they were safely hidden again by the curve of the hill. But Dag was growing fretful and tired, his bright new hopes worn down by his gnawing stomach and his aching legs.

"Why couldn't you have asked them for some bread?" he demanded fretfully. "Will there be something to eat when we get to the south?"

Hungry or not, Merca was terrified of being taken captive once again and did not dare go near a homestead. She could only offer Dag a drink of water from a small stream, where he lay down thirstily among the yellow kingcups that frothed its edges. He forgot his troubles for a few moments when he sat up again, brushing the drifts of yellow pollen off his bare and dirty arms.

By the time the spring twilight came with soft green sky and fluting blackbirds, they found themselves on the edge of a wood, still searching desperately for food, and they had forgotten all about looking for the north. Merca looked at the brambles that reached and climbed with young shoots along the hedges, and thought wistfully of autumn at her home. Then they had picked basket after basket of ripe, dark blackberries, tipping them into the great iron pot swinging over her mother's fire and filling the kitchen with a sour delicious smell. Even a few blackberries would now be a feast, but these brambles held nothing but the unfolding crumple of young leaves and the far promise of harvest to come. The weary girl clung to Dag's hand and began to wonder if she had only led him from a life that was bad to one that was hopeless.

"It will be better when we come to a town, Dag," she comforted him. "We can beg there and we are not so likely to be taken."

Dag's gray eyes, which had grown lively through the freedom of the day, were dull again, and his feet dragged through the thick grass. He did not answer.

Yet it was he who first saw the fire. They were unwilling to go into the darkness of the woods again at night, and walked along the edge of them, hoping to find some way around. Merca had not been paying much attention to the woods themselves, her head up to sniff the air which was filled with some strange familiar clarity, some fresh lightness she had known before. At last she knew it for what it was, her mind going back to the days in Wearmouth.

"Why Dag," she cried, "we are near the sea! I can smell it." Into her mind with the memory of the sea came another memory, long laid aside, of a young princess with red-gold hair and a gentle, lovely face, called Margaret. Merca sighed and pushed it all from her.

"The sea, Dag! You remember the sea, don't you?" Surely he could not have forgotten this too?

Dag was not interested in the sea at the moment. He had stopped and was peering into the woods through the bushes at the edge, and when Merca joined him she also stopped thinking of the sea. Deep into the trees, the trunks and bushes made a dark pattern against the dancing glow of a fire in some clearing in the wood, but they could see no one and nothing save the clear red and yellow flicker of the flames.

"There must be someone there," whispered Merca.

"Perhaps a charcoal burner," Dag said, and Merca glanced at him a moment, surprised by this sudden memory from the forest near their home.

"Someone alone," she went on hopefully. "It does not seem to be a house, but just a fire. Someone alone could not do us much harm."

"And they might have something to eat." Dag finished with the thought that was uppermost in both their minds.

"Come. We'll creep in and see. Quietly now, Dag."

They were as quiet, they thought, as the fox creeping

down on the hen coop in the dawn, stepping silently over the carpet of moss and leaves and treading down the first small flowers of spring, beckoned on by the warm alluring glow of the fire, easing back the branches and under-growth that got in their way until they stood at the edge of a small clearing. The fire blazed merrily in the middle of it, with a pot hissing over it on three sticks, and the air full of the warm smell of burning wood and the sweet savory odors of cooking. To one side of the clearing a hobbled horse plucked at the rich young grass, and before the fire a man was sitting cross-legged, the firelight bright on his dark, crumpled face. His teeth were sunk happily in a whole chicken carcass which he held between his dripping fingers, leaning forward over the fire so that the grease should not fall on his coat. They could not take their eyes off the fowl, their mouths opening and their tongues creeping around their lips. There was something about the easy, relaxed look of the man and his dark, good-natured face that made them forget to be afraid, and they stepped on into the edge of the ring of firelight, hand in hand.

The man did not stop eating, but he raised a pair of bright black eyes above the carcass and took it from his mouth for one short moment.

"You made enough noise in coming," he said, "to rock the dead in stone coffins. But now that you are here, had you better not sit down?"

hey came slowly and dumbly into the close red circle of the fire, and sank down in front of it as he had bidden them. Neither of them could truly remember when they had last felt the warmth of a fire, and the fierce heat was like a blessing on their aching bodies, but the smell of the chicken and of the savory something bubbling in the pot drove them almost frantic, and their wide desperate eyes never left the food in the man's hands.

"If I had need of a pair of scarecrows to scare the birds off my fields," he said, eyeing them over the steaming chicken, "I would look no further. If I had fields," he added almost as an afterthought, but the eyes that looked at them were not unkind, and even as he spoke, he was tearing the two legs off the bird.

"It might be perhaps that you are hungry?" he asked, and the black eyebrows climbed to his hair, as if to show he thought his question ridiculous. But Merca was past humor. She felt her toes curl and her fingers dig into her palms in her effort not to snatch the food from his hands, and beside her she could hear Dag whimpering like a small animal. With a desperate effort, she kept her hands in her lap.

"Dag is hungry," she said faintly. It was just possible that he might not give enough for two.

The man leaned forward and put the two legs of chicken into their frantic fingers, and his eyes resting on Merca were kind but derisive.

54

"And you are not, my little maid? With your bones sticking through the holes in your shift and your eyes fallen in to the back of your head. You are not hungry. Force yourself to eat, then, little one. Force yourself—there is good broth boiling here in the pot from a hare that was unwise enough to cross my path this morning. And if there is anyone from here to Humber makes better broth of a hare than I, then show him to me and I will make a broth of him."

Merca paid no attention, all her mind was on the bone that was being stripped with agonizing speed under her teeth, and only faintly aware of the dark pine trees and of the horse that munched behind them. It was Dag who raised his head to frown over what the man had said.

"It might be a her," he said finally, settling the matter, and the man widened his eyes in splendid amazement.

"It might be a her! Ah, well and truly spoken—it might be a her. Here is wit in this small body as well as a good appetite. Well, we will have a broth of him or her." He turned in high good humor to an earthen jar that stood beside him, taking out the stopper for a long satisfying pull, and sighing with pleasure as he put it back.

Merca was finished, and held her bone hopefully in her hand, terrified to ask for more and yet still frantically hungry, although she could not believe their good fortune in getting as much as they had. The man, however, asked them no questions and seemed quite disinterested in where they had come from or who they were. He seemed to take it quite for granted that he would share with them all he had himself.

"For a maid who is not hungry, you eat quickly! Now, I have but one bowl, but you can share it with the small one here for some of my broth that is hare, but not him or her."

In the silence, Dag laughed suddenly, his rare, short laugh, and Merca turned and stared at him in astonishment, for it was a sound she had long forgotten.

"Ah, me," the man said ruefully, as though delighted that he could amuse them, and yet ashamed of the simplicity of his jest. His eyes rested in tolerant pleasure on Dag's face that was beginning to look almost like itself again in the kindly glow of the firelight with the good, hot food slipping into his stomach. Merca took the bowl, and leaned cautiously over the round pot to dip for the broth, and when she sat back again, the man gave them each a hunk of bread, turning back for another pull at his earthen jar.

Then he sat back and watched them as they huddled together before the fire, dipping their hunks of bread into the same bowl and turning every so often to look at each other with wide, delighted eyes that asked in wonder if this were all really true. Although to the children he seemed very old, he was actually a vigorous thirty years, his square sturdiness not to be seen when he was sitting down. His thick dark hair flowed in unruly curls down to his shoulders, and his features had that odd, blunt look, as if—thought Merca, looking at him—God had not made any of them sharp enough; and his bright good-natured eyes were deep in soft pockets of flesh.

At last Merca felt she had had enough. The blessed

warmth of the fire and the food creeping through her starved body left only exhaustion to dim her eyes and fuddle her senses so that the whole strange setting seemed unreal. The bright fire wavered and leaped and fell, and in its uncertain light the pillared tree trunks came and went through the soft haze of heat, and underneath their shadows the poor quiet horse looked like some strange unearthly monster. She felt Dag's weight sag suddenly against her, and in her weariness she looked down for a moment at his sleeping face, almost as if she did not know who he was. She felt dimly, however, that she had a duty to care for him; to be sure that it was safe for them to stay where they were; to be sure that this stranger would not harm them, though it would seem stupid, said her fuddled mind, to feed them first and then kill them afterward. With drowsy fingers she plucked at her tattered skirt and managed a small smile at the idea that they might have anything to steal. Abruptly she flung up her sinking head and tried to steady her eyes, and fire and man and horse all swirled together with the dark surrounding woodland in her desperate need for sleep.

"What is your name, sir?" she asked as firmly as she could, and added from some long lost habit, "We thank you for our supper."

Feverishly blinking to keep open her collapsing eyelids, she watched him take another pull from the earthen jar, and then he shook it irritably as if it were growing empty. Putting it down again among the saddlebags, he leaned over to her confidentially, wiping his mouth on the back of his two hands, one after the other.

57

"My name, little maid?" He seemed to feel it was something that he had reason to be very proud of, and she struggled to pay attention. In his efforts to come so close that she would be sure to hear him, he had toppled over onto his elbow and now lay looking up at her, his odd crumpled face crimson in the firelight, his long hair dangling to the grass. A moment of fear trembled in her but she was too far gone in weariness to acknowledge it, and she just accepted him as he was, unreal and strange like all the rest of this shimmering night.

"Thomas," he said, and pride filled his voice as he spoke. "Thomas of the Knife they call me, for I prefer the knife."

"The knife?" she asked stupidly, thinking it must be something to do with the way he ate his food.

"The knife," he said again, contentedly. "Although," he added as one who gave fair thought to everything, "to suffocate them has its merits, when time and place are right. It is silent, see you, and that means much, in my trade."

It made no sense, any of it, all part of a dream like everything else, and she did her best to sort it out through the clouds of threatening sleep.

"What is the knife for?" He had given them his food, and some old, half-forgotten teaching made Merca feel that because of this it was her duty to talk with him courteously if he wanted to talk. He did want to talk, but first he reached again for the earthen jar, and she heard him hiccup as he leaned back close to her.

"The knife?" To kill, of course, what else?" His voice

was low now, almost whispering, and his face glowed with a moody, indrawn pleasure, as if he thought of things that pleased him. Merca shivered abruptly, and felt distantly that if she were more awake, she would be very frightened. Whom did he kill? And why? She asked him, and he looked at her in the unstable light as if he thought she must be a little simple.

"For gold, of course, my little maid! What else is worth doing anything for. Oh, you can keep your high thoughts of love and duty, and this and thus, but Thomas is not that kind of simpleton, and works only for gold. And if you have an enemy and wish him dead, and have the gold to pay, then Thomas of the Knife is the man for you. Quick I am, but silent, and I have never failed." His rosy face was bright with pride in his own skill, but as Merca watched him and tried to believe what he had said, she saw the glow of pride fade, to be replaced by one of sadness, and Thomas sighed heavily, and shook his head. "Many years, though, I have been working at my trade and always given satisfaction, yet I have never reached the top of it." He turned again to the earthen jar, and took a pull at it; then he looked over at another that lay among his packs. It was too much effort to reach it, and he turned back to the girl who was watching him from under falling lids as if he had laid a spell on her.

"Thegns," he said sadly, wiping his mouth. "Thegns and jarls and all kinds of people in high places, for these are the ones who have most enemies and earn their death for their ambitions, though never have I done the one thing that any man like me would want to do. Not only for the gold, you know, even though that would be the finest sum. But also to say to myself that I have done it. To remember what it felt like."

It appeared he had forgotten he was talking to anyone except himself, his eyes wide and full of longing, and Merca made her last effort, shifting Dag's inert body a little so that she might be more comfortable.

"What is it you want to do?" she asked him, and sleep swept her so that she could scarcely move her lips. "What is so important?"

Far and loud and strange she heard the answer booming in her head as she abandoned all her struggles and let sleep claim her. Her eyes closed and she could no longer see him.

"To kill a king!" she heard him say, and his yearning voice echoed round and round in the dizzy mists into which she fell. "To kill a king! Think of the gold and think of the pride of it! I want to kill a king!"

Then Merca collapsed into a heap on top of Dag, and heard no more, but somewhere above her in her dreams there hovered the clear picture of the great evil, red-whiskered face of the King of Scotia. Malcolm, King of Scotia.

Long habit beat down her weariness and it was dawn when she awoke, with the gray light growing between the straight trunks of the pines and the whole wood alive with the chittering and fluting of the morning birdsong. The long grass was cold and silver under dew and the fresh chilly air sharp with the tang of larch and spruce, and for a moment she lay and breathed the sweet morning, remembering with a surge of excitement that they were free. Dag was still asleep as indeed he always had been, leaving it to her to rouse them every morning in time to escape the inevitable beating if their Mistress should be the first to wake and find them not already at work. She sat up quietly now not wishing to disturb the man who slept beyond the ash-heaped fire, rolled in a cloak of faded blue. His sprawled legs stuck out foolishly, in coarse cloth hose, cross-gartered into soft leather shoes. Until she had time to think a little she did not want to wake him, her still drowsy mind struggling with the strangest memories of talk last night in the darkness.

Remembering more, she sat up at once briskly and the last waves of sleep slipped from her mind as she looked at him closely. He seemed harmless enough, snoring away there beneath his cloak, the new earthen jar close beside his hand and his queer face looking even simpler and more kind in sleep than it had done when he was awake. For a brief moment she thought of waking Dag and creeping quietly away, but she was hungry again and her stomach nagged to stay, whatever the man might be, lest he have more food. Watching him, his last words of the night flared again in her mind, just as they had edged her dreams.

"To kill a king," he had said. "I want to kill a king!"

So there were men like this, she thought, who would take a life if they were paid enough. It must be so, when you are in high place and wish to rid yourself of your enemies; there must be someone to do it. She was not surprised, for she had learnt much and grown older since the evening when she had found smoke rising above the gutted thatch of her home, and nothing any longer surprised her. Dag was heavy against her side and she moved away a little to stretch her cramped and chilly limbs. Dag moved after her at once, like a small animal seeking warmth, and looking down at his thin face, the thought of the burly King of Scots came between her and the brightening day, and her mouth set and sharpened purposefully as she stared again at the man across the fire. Quietly she put Dag aside.

When the man at last stirred and woke, muttering and grumbling, and licking around his parched mouth, she had already rekindled the fire with dry wood she had found by pottering around the edges of the clearing, her face brushed by the green fingers of the larches, and her ankles stung by the cold dew-drenched grass. She was near to happiness as she bent to fill the skin water bag at a small brown sparkling stream, and came back to set the black pot boiling above the new fire. The man was confused when he awoke, and seemed to take a little time to remember where he was, rumpling his hair until it curled down over his forehead like a bull, and shaking himself with violent, angry shudders. She watched patiently and waited, until he reached and took a drink from the earthen jar, and seemed then to recover, but still he looked at her as if he remembered her, but faintly. Merca looked at him anxiously, knowing now what he was, but she clasped her hands in her lap and hung on to her courage, for she was determined not to run away. She had business with this man.

It was a good start that he was pleased about the fire.

"Good, my little maid, and clever," he said, and leaned to rub his hands thankfully before the blaze. To the watching girl it looked as if he gathered the pieces of himself together and, before her eyes again became a whole man. "You have earned your morning meal, but what about this lie-abed over here?" He reached out a foot and poked at Dag, who grumbled in his sleep but did not stir. The man laughed.

"I do not blame you, little brother! Stay asleep! There is little in this world to get up for. Now, my small maid, we will make the heathen food of this country where we are." From a bag he heaped fistfuls of coarse brown oatmeal into the pot that Merca had ready bubbling over the fire. "It looks most horrible and tastes no better, but it is warm against the stomach and lasts a man well on a journey. They tell me these barbarous Scots carry it cold in bags, and eat a lump off it when they are hungry. Ugh!"

Merca nodded, for she had seen the soldiers do this, and had known the days when her famished stomach had had nothing more than the heavy welcome weight of a lump of cold porridge. But now her mind was on what the man had said about Dag, and she grasped it to lead on to her purpose.

"Why did you say to my brother that there is nothing to get up for?" she asked him, and her heart hammered with nervousness as she tried to manage what she wanted to say. "You do not find that your life, your—trade—is good?"

63

He looked at her sharply as he stirred the porridge with a piece of stick.

"What do you know about my trade?" he asked her, and his voice was no longer slow and lazy. For a moment she was frightened, facing a different man with a tight mouth and hard black eyes, and she wished she had taken Dag and gone, but there was something here that she must do, and although she shook inside and trembled right down through her legs, she held her ground and met him bravely eye to eye.

"What you told me, sir, yourself, last night. Surely it can be no secret what you do, or how would men find you when they needed you? How would you get your work?"

This seemed to amuse him, and he began to laugh, the taut face relaxing and the good humor returning to the eyes.

"True, my little one, true. True indeed. Men come from all the country over for the services I can render."

Merca asked him something that had been puzzling her ever since they first came into the clearing and the man spoke to them in Saxon.

"You are not a Scot?"

"I am not a Scot. I am a Saxon, but from the far west where the mountains rise and men are dark of hair and skin." His face clouded again, broody over the thick, lumpy porridge which he dipped out into the one bowl. Almost fiercely, he turned on her. "But Saxon or Scot, I am no man's liege, be he Saxon himself or conquering Norman or beetling Scot. I am my own lord and my own life, and I live for myself, no man commanding me unless he commands my knife with gold." He thrust the porridge bowl at her. "Here, take this, lest you may never see another."

Even as she blew on the steaming porridge and supped at it, thinking it poor and lumpy and half cooked and that the woman would have beaten her back sore for such a boiling, her mind was circling desperately around the one vital thing she wished to ask him. In the end she came flat out with it, breathlessly, and directly.

"How much would you charge? How much would it cost to have someone very—important—disposed of?"

The man roared with laughter, his face creasing up almost into nothing so that his eyes were lost in folded caverns of flesh, and across the fire Dag stirred.

"How much gold would I need to kill someone important? What is that to you, small scarecrow? What know you of gold or of important people?"

Merca was nettled, angry to be so dismissed when the hate that boiled in her was great enough to make her do the deed herself, had she only the strength, and would be enough, surely, in time, to drive her on to find the gold to get it done.

"Why do you laugh?" she burst out angrily. "Why do you laugh? Might I not be the one to ask you to kill a king?"

He was wiping tears of mirth from his eyes, and this remark almost set him off again, but he looked at her with painful gravity and took the empty bowl from her hands.

"To be sure, little maid, you might!" he said. "To be sure you might. But for now, what about some porridge for blubber face, waking over there."

Merca looked indignantly at Dag's poor bony face.

"He is no blubber face! How can you say so?"

"Perhaps not now," the man agreed amiably, "but he has the look to me that if someone fed him up, he could become one. Here boy, make a start with this."

Only then, as Dag supped noisily at his porridge, did he begin to ask them anything at all about themselves, listening to all Merca told him with an irritated frown, as though he found it hard that things like these should befall a pair of children. But, after all, it was nothing to do with him. As Merca finished speaking, he got up and went over the grass to give his horse a bag of oats, stepping delicately—like a cat—as if he were afraid of the dew on his soft shoes.

"And what now?" he asked, coming back and standing over them like a man who is ready to depart. "What now? Where are you making for?"

Dag wiped his porridge-covered mouth carefully on the rags that had once been a shirt sleeve.

"We are going to the south," he announced firmly, and the man turned to Merca with raised eyebrows. Carefully she explained how she hoped to lead Dag back close to their own home, and Thomas of the Knife nodded.

"The best thing," he agreed. "The best thing. And you will not be troubled in Northumbria for a while, for all I hear of Malcolm Canmore is that he is keeping close at home in his palace of Dunfermline, with a new wife, lost for the moment to the arts of war. Well—I'll tell you what. I am riding north in search of trouble, for where trouble lies, then there lies work for Thomas. But I will set you on the road to the south before I leave you." He seemed pleased with this decision, as if it covered all his responsibilities.

"Thank you, sir," said Merca, and "Thank you, sir," echoed Dag, looking a little doubtfully at his porridge bowl, as though surprised to find it empty.

Merca was puzzled by the man Thomas. He seemed to be a wanderer like themselves, only with everything he needed for his wayside life strung in packs about his horse. Yet for all his way of life, there was something in the way he moved and spoke that made her grope back into the days when she knew of manners to call him sir.

He answered their thanks easily. "It is nothing. It is nothing. Are we not vagabonds together?"

They watched while he neatly stowed all his belongings into the packs that hung against his horse's flanks, taking one last pull at the earthen flask before he hooked it onto his saddle.

"What is in there?" Dag asked him curiously. "Is it water?"

"You might say so, little brother," he answered. "You might say so. The water of life, they call it. Aqua vitae," he said, and they did not understand him, but dimly Merca understood that she should be grateful to this water of life for making him so talkative the night before, or she might never have learned his trade.

He left them at a broad track that led along the slope of a hill through the stiff ranked pines, and told them that if they followed it, it would bring them out onto a small road. On this, they must turn to the right, and that would start them on their way southward. He told them how to watch the sun and keep the east, where it rose, always to their left hand, and then they would have their faces towards the south.

"But you must," he insisted, "turn to the right when you come out onto the road." He looked at Merca. "Do you know which is your right hand?"

"Of course," she said loftily. "Of course."

"Good. Then I bid you farewell and good fortune."

He bade them farewell as easily as he had first greeted them, riding away without a backward glance, and they stood for a long time watching him; the blue of his receding cloak deepening in the shadows of the trees, and his bundles bobbing on his horse's flanks. Only then did Merca remember that she had forgotten to ask how men got in touch with him if they wanted something done, but she shrugged and was not much troubled. The gold came first and that might take a very long time.

Exactly as he had said, they came out between the young green spikes of the pines onto the road, dry after the fine weather, rutted with the marks of unshod wheels and pitted and beaten by the hooves of horses. It stretched away from them on either side, between the dusky woodland and the fields; to the left and to the right. Dag stood and waited in silent confidence, for had not Merca told the man that she knew her right hand.

68

Merca made a sudden equally confident gesture with her hands and then stopped and looked at them in dismay, turning piteous eyes on Dag.

"Oh, Dag!" She looked down at her hands again, and she hardly knew how to tell him. "Oh, Dag, I *did* know my right hand. It is the one with which you make the Sign of the Cross—this our mother taught me. But it is so long since I have said a prayer or blessed myself that I have forgotten which is the hand to use. I do not know my left hand from my right and we still cannot see the sun."

CHAPTER SIX

There was nothing to do but hope for the best.

"Did you understand all that he said about the sun, Dag?"

Dag shook his head, for he had not even listened, certain that Merca would look after everything. He was feeling a little better now, safer, and his stomach was full, so that his dulled eyes were beginning to look around again and see the things they rested on, struck with pleasure by the dark straight columns of the trees, and the tender green of the young wheat that looked almost as if it had been smeared over the fields across the road. Once more, these things filled his mind and he could not worry about where the sun was, or that Merca did not know her right hand from her left.

Merca sighed and gave up; what use was it, even if they could remember what the man said? She looked hopelessly up and down the empty road.

"This way, Dag," she said firmly, and started off in the direction that led slightly downhill, Dag following her quite contentedly, trying to place his feet in the dried-up shapes of horses' hoofs, and sniffing at the rich springtime smell of the countryside, laid over unmistakably with the sharp tang of the sea.

Merca sniffed too.

"We must be getting closer to the water," she said, puzzled, for they could not see it. Their road, winding along in a slight depression between green banks starred with the soft yellow of the primrose, with the bare twigs fringed above them by dancing catkins, gave no warning of the moment when there was suddenly a space between the trees and the grassy edges fell away into nothing. Down and down it fell, to the far floor of the blue spring-time sea, which crinkled in the light wind and then smoothed away again into a sheen of silk, the sails of ships looking no bigger than Merca's thumbnail. With infinite care, for they could not remember having been so high before, they crept on their hands and knees to the edges of the grass, peering over the cliff to see what lay below.

"It is a town," cried Merca in amazement, for there did not seem to be room for anything between the dizzy clifftops and the sea.

Dag thumped his feet behind him with pleasure, and Merca grabbed him lest he fall.

"There we will get food," he cried in unusual enthusi-asm. "Now we will be safe, sister! You said it would be better when we reached a town."

Merca herself could not resist being excited, for it seemed to her that in a town lay their only hope, and they had found one before they were even properly hungry again after the good feeding of Thomas of the Knife. In great high spirits they slipped and slithered down the narrow path that led down the face of the cliff.

In the small town at the bottom they did indeed suc-ceed in begging half enough to keep them for a few days, for now they could speak the Gaelic they had learned at the farm and need not draw attention to themselves with their slow Saxon speech. The weather grew fine and warm

for them and they washed themselves in the sea, rags and all, and sat on the pebbly shore to stare at each other in amazement until Merca shrieked with laughter, and even Dag rumbled his slow sedate laugh at the sight of the pale, clean skins they had not seen for over a year. At night they slept on the shore in the shelter of an old boat, and they knew a spell of safety and only half hunger, but it did not last them long. The town they had found was a small one and they soon found they had exhausted its charity for the people lived on their meager earnings from the sea and had little enough for their own needs. After a short while, even those who had at first looked with pity on their starving faces and given them a lump of porridge or a piece of fish, began to glare at them in anger and hostility and threaten to drive them from the town.

"We must move on, Dag." Merca was urgent, for the town seemed even more dangerous than the lonely country, and she was growing very tired. It had seemed a brave thing to her to take Dag and run away from the farm and make a new life for them both, but she knew now that she had not really considered whether there was anywhere to run to. They were as far as ever from the south or even knowing how to get there. She was beginning to be afraid that she and Dag would be on the road forever, until the struggle for food should grow too great. In the end they would be just two more bundles of rags beside the road, like the many they had left on the trail north with the soldiers. The weather had forsaken them too. A cold rain soaked their wretched clothes, and Dag lost the small burst of spirit with which he had greeted the sight of the town. It was in dead silence that she took his hand and set off in the rain along the shore, too frightened to go back toward the town.

There were then days and nights that she barely remembered afterward. All firm idea of finding the south, or indeed of going anywhere at all were now forgotten, and, finding the road again, they struck inland blindly. But the narrow track ran always with the smell and feeling of the sea and, often, on high ground within sight of it, blue or gray, and hazy in the distance against the far shadows of rounded purple hills. They were soaked with hours of bitter mist that blinded them to everything except the road in front of their feet and flattened their drenched rags against their bones and chilled their hungry bodies. They slept as best they could under hedges or in the long grass, begging a bite from any traveler they chanced to meet, but happening much more frequently on kicks and curses than on a crust of bread. Starving, they crept one night through the shadowed moonlight to try to raid a henhouse, desperate for the eggs to suck, but they made poor thieves and roused the household, so that they had to fly in terror from a bedlam of squawking hens and barking dogs and kindled lights. When at last all grew quiet behind them and they dared to stop, they were still starving, but worn out now with running.

They were too terrified and shaken even to think of sleeping, and Merca had now become certain that if she should stop to rest, she would never start again. Dag was past protesting about anything, so she led him all that night along a country track under the declining moon, light-headed with hunger and fatigue so that she no longer knew exactly what she did. Dag plodded in silence beside her, the only reality being the clasp of their hands in a world of darkness and cold and hunger that somehow did not seem to matter any more.

Dawn found them in a softly wooded country, their road following a slight rise of land beyond which they could not see. Not that Merca cared what might lie beyond it. The first rays of the morning sun struck flat down the grassy slope and fell warm and full on their faces, and it was this touch of the sun that brought her to a halt.

"Dag," she said. She knew there was a great deal she should say to him, for Dag knew nothing, and how could he live alone? "Dag," she said again, and turned to try and speak to him, but his face slid queerly from side to side and changed suddenly in a rush of darkness into the monstrous swelling face of Malcolm, King of Scotia, who had brought them to all this. The hate inside her head was like the roaring of a black sea, coming between her and the sunlight, and between her and little Dag, who could not live without her. He tried to catch her as she slid to the ground in the middle of the track, but he was too small.

They were found by a company on horseback who, later in the morning, came riding from the woods towards the ridge of the hill. Merca still lay where she had fallen and, beside her, Dag sat on the muddy track like a small silent watchdog, his eyes dark pools of determination and fright and his fingers flying frantically round the curves of his shell. He sat unmoving and watched them come, and did not know what to expect—certainly not that they would rein in their horses and circle round him, with the ladies uttering sharp cries of pity and concern. It was so long since he had met with pity that he stared in dumb surprise as one of the gentlemen, in a woolen cap and a gay checkered cloak, leapt at once from his horse and bent over Merca. Then Dag came to life.

"Leave her alone!" he cried, and struck out fiercely at the bright cap that tried to come near his sister.

"Peace, little son," the young man said and laughed, turning away the small, flailing fist. "I will not harm her."

Dag did not believe him. In the only world that he knew now, people did not want to help him, especially people in fine clothes who spoke a queer mixture of Gaelic and Saxon in clear voices somewhere up in the sky above him. He flung himself down on top of Merca, nor would he move for all the man's beguiling.

"It's no use," he said in the end, getting up. "Here, Mary, I'll hand you down and you speak with him. They're both starving by the look of it."

Somewhere in the bright sky a girl laughed.

"Yes, let me try. Those whiskers are enough to frighten anyone, Dougal."

Dag heard the soft thump of her feet on the road as she slid from her horse, but even when she came close she did not speak to him. He could feel her beside him, crouching in the roadway, so that out of the corner of his curious eye he could see the dust marking the flowing crimson of her skirts, and he could smell a nice, sweet smell that he had

76

never met before. He felt a gentle arm go round him and a hand moving softly through his hair, just as some other hand had done, somewhere, sometime; but still she did not speak to him, but went on talking to the man across his head. Dag could see the rough cloth of his trews and the leather thongs of his cross gartering where he knelt again quite close beside his head.

"Starving," said the girl, and her soft voice was full of pity. "Both of them, but the girl is more desperate. Strange, Dougal, is it not, that one of the Queen's seven should have died, and so new come to her too, and then we find these on the same morning as if they had been sent to take the dead child's place?"

Dougal's voice was more practical and a little doubting.

"But there are two of them, and there is only place for one. And truly, Mary my sister, we do not have to come out and seek paupers for the Queen to care for. There are plenty close at hand."

"The Queen will see to all that," the girl said comfortably. "She will not separate them, but for now we must get them back with us."

Dag did not know it, but under the caressing hand and the gentle voice that soothed him with a sense of safety even while it did not speak to him directly, he had been losing all his defenses. The blind wall he had built up against the long, long months of misery and want began to collapse. Suddenly he fell on top of his sister, his rigid little body gone soft with the tears he had held back so long, nor did he protest when the girl lifted him up and beckoned one of the servants who rode behind her.

"Merca," was all he managed to say, and the tears ran down into his mouth. "Sister."

"Yes, yes, we will take your sister too."

In a matter of moments they were in front of two men servants on their horses, the girl turning her veiled head frequently to look with anxiety at Merca, and to give a warm sweet, reassuring smile to Dag. Slowly his sobs hiccupped to a stop, and as if to reassure himself that something was the same in this wonderfully changing world, he opened his hot, damp hand and looked at the shell in his palm. But he had no energy for his fingers to move round its curves and he closed his fist on it again. Under his head he could feel the smooth slip and creak of the man's leather jerkin easing with the movements of his horse, and the firm grip of strong arms was comfortable around his waist. The horse was strong and solid under his legs and the sun struck warm on his face, and he was fast asleep long before they reached the crest of the ridge and looked down on a steep glen like a sword cut through the green hills, with a sprawl of wattle buildings perched along its edge.

everal times in the next days, Merca awoke a little, swimming up out of the warm, drowsy haze that submerged her in some delightful dream of comfort and firelight and sometimes candlelight, and kind quiet voices speaking close beside her. Once she swam up uncertainly into the most beautiful dream of them all, and thought impossibly that she saw bending over her the lovely and gentle face of the girl she had watched coming in from the ship in Wearmouth; a look of tender concern in her blue eyes and the light behind her making a halo of her softly curling red-gold hair. She understood that none of this could be true, but mercifully each time before the reality of cold and hunger could take her again, or her gnawing anxiety about Dag, the mists of sleep would close into soft darkness and she would sink down once more into nothing.

At last she woke completely to find it evening, and struggled from the depths of days of sleep to look around her in bewilderment, staring slowly from the pile of wolf and sheepskins on her soft bed to the glowing fire in the middle of the floor, and the other beds against the walls, several of them, like long wooden boxes filled with straw and piled with skins and woolen covers. There was an unshuttered window in the wattle wall opposite her, the square opening filled with the deep purple sky of the late day and one solitary star offering its pale glimmer against the steady light of a candle on a table near the fire; and from somewhere close at hand she could hear the rush and scutter of quick footsteps, and the sound of children laughing. In slow confusion she looked all around her and then looked down at the woolen robe she was wearing, marveling dumbly at the rich embroidery on the cuffs. Then memory came rushing back and with it fear and terrible loneliness that banished the warmth and candle-light and the one friendly star.

"Dag!" she screamed. "Dag!" She tried desperately to struggle from the deep bed, but her limbs were strangely weak and soft and as if in a dream of terror, she could not manage to move. Again and again she called, sitting bolt upright to stare with wide, frightened eyes at the girl who came running in answer.

"Dag," she said again, hoarsely, and the girl took her outstretched hands, sinking to the edge of the bed in a sweep of bright striped skirts, her dark face alive with pleasure.

"So you are awake! And better? Madam the Queen will be pleased." Although Merca did not know it, it was the same dark girl who had climbed from her horse to talk to Dag in the middle of the road, her shining black hair uncovered now, braided but a little ruffled around a high-boned cheerful face. "Rest now, my sweeting, and I will bring you something to eat, for I wager you are hungry. Do not try to sit up."

Merca fought her gentle hands, her thin face still sharp with fright.

"Dag," was all she could say. "Where is Dag?"

Light dawned on the girl's rosy face and an odd amused smile.

"The little brother?" she asked. "His name is Dag? He has not told us. But do not fret about him, for he is here and well and I will bring him back with me when I bring the broth."

Gratefully Merca sank back against the blue and scarlet bolsters that the girl snatched from other beds to pile behind her.

"Where am I?" she asked weakly, but she did not bother very much about the answer. Nor did the girl give her one as she arranged the bright pillows to her comfort.

"My name is Mary," was all she said. "I am one of the Queen's ladies and I help to look after all her children such as you, and even though now by God's good grace she has her own baby son, she loves them not one whit less."

Merca was too weary to think any of it out, her mind as worn as her starved body, and she could not even manage to be curious as to who this queen was or what children she cared for. For the moment she was willing to accept the miracle that they had found someone who would care for them; more she did not question.

Nor had Dag questioned anything. He came as Mary had promised, following her in when she brought the bowl of steaming broth, and for a long time his sister stared at him and almost did not know him, wondering if it was a trick of the candlelight on his face and hair that made him already look almost like the old bland, contented Dag.

"He can stay and talk to you a little," Mary said when Merca turned her tired head away after sipping a very little of the broth, her eyes all the time on the strange, clean, smooth-haired little brother who crouched on the bottom of the bed. "But not for long, for you must sleep again."

Indeed her eyelids seemed weighted with the darkness of the evening, and struggled to collapse again over her drowsy eyes, but she must keep awake long enough to talk to Dag.

"Dag, where are we?"

Dag shrugged his shoulders. "I do not know, sister. I do not know." He looked at her as though he thought her foolish to care. "There is much to eat, and they have given me a new tunic with a pouch at the waist, see, that holds my shell. It can hold money too, whenever I get some. Gold perhaps." He fingered lovingly at the soft leather of his little pouch, and Merca smiled to see him so happy, but a fragment of her sleepy mind jumped back to remember the man in the clearing and her own driving need for gold. She wondered if this was a place where she might be able to get some. How was it possible to get gold? She was too tired to think of it and turned again to Dag.

"Who is here, Dag, besides the lady who is called Mary? Who do you see?"

"Many ladies, and a few gentlemen who come in sometimes, and there are many children too. You can hear them."

"Whose children?"

"I don't know. The Queen calls us all her children when she comes to have breakfast with us in the morn-

ing." His face puckered. "But we cannot all be her children since you and I once had a mother of our own." He
was silent a moment, impressed by his own reasoning.
"There is a boy called Duncan, but I do not like him; he
is rough and took my shell. There are two ladies who
come in, too." He glanced at Merca doubtfully as he said
this and wondered if he should go on.

He had shed his troubles easily, and having had a full
stomach for a few days he was well content to forget the
past and let it go. Merca did not notice his hesitation
and she was too weak to sort out anything he said, lying
gratefully back on the colored pillows, savoring her warm
bed and the comfort of it, and watching the square of sky
darken into night, the candle and the one star melting
into blobs of radiance under her drowsy eyes. One light
of silver, she thought hazily, and one of gold. Gold for
vengeance. She did not know the word vengeance, but
she knew the hard fierce feeling that swept her even
thinking of the King of Scotia, and knowing that gold
was all that was needed to bring about his death. She
did not forget her injuries as easily as Dag, but her mind
was not yet clear and jumped from one thing to another,
the thought of a king leading her back to the queen.

"This queen you all speak of," she said drowsily. "Who
is she? What is she queen of?"

Dag shrugged again. He did not listen much to the
people talking around him. Now that he was no longer
starving, his eyes were on the things that interested him;
the trees that rose up the steep sides of the glen below
the palace, the unfolding green of the alders and the

birches against the dark winter shadows of the pines, and on the breath-snatching colors in something this pretty queen had shown him which she called a book. It was full of strange black markings called letters, with bigger marks twined with flowers and little animals in colors and shining pieces of gold that she had let him touch just once with a clean finger. This was all called writing. These things took Dag's mind, along with the odd, un-even singing of a crowd of men in black robes who knelt in a great wattle hall they called the church. It was lit with many candles and was always filled with a strange and pleasant silence. These things he liked and noticed, but he could not speak of them.

"But sister," he said then, a little proud of himself that he could tell her something. "There is something about this queen, and you will find it very strange. Do you remember when we were in that place beside the sea before the soldiers took us away and I dropped my shell? Well . . ." Even Dag's steady voice was warming to inter-est at this strange story, but he faltered to a stop. Merca was fast asleep, her dark lashes fanned out over cheeks still as pale as the sheepskins that covered her, and Dag sighed deeply, for he so rarely had something to say, and it was such an effort to say it. Then he leaned over and kissed her and went stolidly out, leaving her to the star-light and the candlelight and the shifting fire shadows on the wattle walls.

She did not hear the other children coming to their beds where they slept two and three together, huddled like puppies in the straw beneath their warm skins; seven little orphans of whom Merca herself would be the eldest, taken from poverty and want by the charity of the queen, to be reared in the palace as if they were her own. Only from now on there would be eight, for the lady Mary had read the queen's mind truly when she guessed that she would neither turn Merca away, nor would she separate her from Dag, who was still small enough for a little while to live among the women.

The next morning Merca woke before the dawn to lie in weak content in the dead half-light, listening to the steady ringing of a bell and the sound of footsteps in the court beyond her window, through which she could see the pale glow of tapers carried in the near darkness. In a little while she heard men singing in a music as flat and dead as the morning light, and realized they must be monks. Across the room she saw Dag sit up suddenly, thrusting aside the child who slept with him, and his eyes were wide and listening as his fingers moved wraptly around his shell. He and the men's voices and the morning hazed into one and she slept again, not to wake until the room was full of streaming sunshine and the chattering of children and the reality of her most lovely dream.

"She is awake and well?" Merca heard a sweet and somehow familiar voice beyond the chamber door. "Well then, let me have her broth, dearest Mary, and I will help her today. She is the newest come and may be lonely, despite the funny little brother."

Puzzled, Merca groped in her memory for the voice, which she was sure she had heard before, but she was not yet capable of much effort and let her mind slide idly away until she lifted startled eyes to find the same lovely face beside her bed as had looked down at her so pityingly on that far distant day beside the sea in Wearmouth.

"Margaret," she whispered in amazement, and her eyes rested wonderingly on the fair, blue-eyed face framed in the soft hair that Dag had so truly likened to the beech trees in the autumn. "Margaret!"

Beside the queen the lady Mary clicked her tongue and her long mouth was disapproving.

"You must speak to the Queen as Madam," she said reproachfully, but the queen only smiled and Merca did not even glance at Mary, unable to take her eyes from this vision which she still half thought to be a dream.

"The soldier told me, 'Margaret,' " she said confusedly, as the queen sat on a stool beside the bed, and took the broth from Mary. Her skirts flowed round her in a surge of purple so brilliant that it almost dazzled the girl who had known only rags and hodden gray for so long.

"What soldier, little daughter?" she asked, and Merca stared, still bemused, thinking that never had she seen such beauty and such gentleness. "What soldier? But first take some of this good broth that you may grow strong again and rush about the glen with your small brother and the other children."

Obediently Merca sipped at the wooden spoon, for she would have done anything on earth that she was asked by this beautiful queen or princess or whoever she might be.

"Enough?" the queen asked then. "It is enough?" and Merca nodded her head.

"It was the soldier in Wearmouth," she said, longing to talk to the soft, sympathetic face. "In Wearmouth, where you got off a ship, and walked to the monks' house, and Dag dropped his shell in front of you. Then the soldiers took us."

The fair face grew puzzled and the brows drew down over the queen's eyes, and, to the watching child, it seemed as if her face grew sad and shadowed with some sorrow bigger than her own. She turned and handed the bowl to the waiting Mary, and Merca tried desperately to dispel that look and make the queen smile again.

"You were very kind to us," she said urgently. "Very kind. The soldier told us that it was because of that—" She would not say Malcolm's name. "That we were not killed. I asked him who you were, and he said you were a princess—but I only remembered Margaret," she added lamely, and blushed all over her thin face to have been so familiar with a queen.

She was rewarded in that the queen did smile again, and took her bony hand inside her own.

"Tell me," she said then gently. "Tell me all of it. About the soldier who spoke my name, and how you came to be alone and starving in Wearmouth as I saw you."

"You remember us?" Merca cried, and the queen nodded, and again the smile had left her face. Eagerly Merca began to pour out their whole story, but she did not manage to get very far. It was the first time since she had lost her home that she had told her story to a face of tenderness; the man called Thomas in the wood had listened with the interest of one vagabond in another and no more. Now as she began to speak, telling of her home and how she and Dag had come from the forest in the evening to find the smoking ruin and the dead mother lying across the lintel of the door, she found she could not tell it to those pitying eyes. Inside the queen's warm grasp, her hand suddenly began to shake until the shaking took hold of her from her head down to her feet and somehow suddenly she was in the queen's arms, weeping as she had not wept even once since that dreadful evening, and through her grief she wondered dimly why it was that the queen wept almost as bitterly as she.

She was tired afterward and wildly happy, as if she had at last laid down some dreadful burden. She lay there in sweet contentment, thinking of the promise that she should never have to go away again, but would stay in the queen's household with the other orphans, and when she was stronger she could learn to weave and sew and cook, until she might in time grow to be one of the queen's own waiting ladies. Warmed and soothed and lapped at last in a sense of complete safety, she was still too exhausted to question very much. The queen was there, incredibly, her own beautiful Margaret, whose memory had lit a small glow in the darkest days of captivity, and she said the name over and over to herself as she had done in the long hours of the march north. "Margaret." It did not occur to her to think in her happy, weary trance, her brain still stupid with starvation, that there must be some connection between this loving queen and the king who was the object of her vengeance. Nor did Dag try again to tell her that the palace they lived in seemed to belong to the King of Scotia. He had tried once and would not make the effort again, for he had other things to think of.

He came to see her in the hour of the midday meal, full of his own new life.

"I have been in the place where the monks live," he said at once.

"Monastery," said Merca, for this she had learned, asking about the singing in the silent morning, and Mary had told her of the thirteen men of the Order of St. Benedict who had followed Queen Margaret to Scotland to found a monastery. She was not very interested. "Dag," she said, "do you not remember seeing the Queen before? We saw her in Wearmouth, when you lost your shell. Do you not remember? I knew her at once—she must have been here before, but I thought it was a dream. Why did you not tell me?"

Dag opened his mouth and shut it again. He could only think of one thing at a time, and now he was full of his own affairs, and he did not answer her.

"I have been in this place," he said again firmly, and Merca looked at him in some surprise, a little more awake today and puzzled by a look of secret joy that she had never seen before on Dag's smooth face. "I have been in this place, and there are men there in long black robes, with their hair cut in a ring about the tops of their heads."

"Monks," said Merca, and thought again of the Feast of Christmas that Dag did not remember.

90

"I know," said Dag patiently, and plowed on. He had a lot to say.

"They told me," he said, staring at his sister with eyes as big and dark as pools, "that if I am good and work hard, they will teach me how to make pictures on— parchment." He struggled for the unfamiliar word. "Pictures like in the Queen's book. In red and blue and gold and black, the colors are all there in little pots of stone, and they put them on with a brush. They will teach me all the letters, they said, and someday I can write myself."

Merca did not quite understand, but she could see that Dag was blazing with some new happiness and that was all that mattered. Like everything else, she was content to let it drift along on the tide of her new safety and contentment, with her warm, soft bed and plenty to eat and her beloved Queen Margaret close at hand, and the future beckoning as warm and safe as the present.

"And when I know the letters," Dag was adding, and his shell was moving slowly between his fingers under his abstracted eyes, "then I can know what it says in books. All books. It seems there are many in the world."

Once again he sighed and turned away, for once again Merca was not listening to him, caught by this treacherous tide of sleep that could still sweep over her despite all the brilliance of the sunshine flooding through the window, and the chattering of the children gathering for their meal in the room beyond, and the bell ringing steadily for the noon Office.

The next morning it roused her again in the first

light of morning, but now she did not feel the need to sleep. This morning she woke to a new feeling of strength and clear-headedness. For all her pleading, the lady Mary would not let her leave her bed, and she watched for the first time with envy as all the others began rolling out of their skins, playing and chasing around the two chambers as the day brightened and the sun streamed in to catch life and color from the bolsters and the snowy sheepskins against the dull shadows of the wattle walls. Mary flew among them, tossing up the rushes and the sprigs of heather with her hasty feet, trying to round them up and urge them to haste as the bang and rattle of the servants putting up the trestles for the morning meal sounded from the next chamber. She seemed to be more than usually urgent, and lined them up giggling before her, three small boys and three small girls, and Dag, to insist that hands were clean and hair neatly braided, and tunics straight and not rumpled through their belts. Merca looked in amazement at the clean and shining Dag who stood beside her bed, but was still too happily indolent to ask him the reason for all this special commotion. Nor would Dag have known if she had asked him, she thought with a spasm of affectionate irritation. Now if she had wanted to know the color of some flower . . .!

She began to listen more closely when she realized that the queen had not come alone to breakfast with her children this morning. Against her soft, sweet voice there was the heavy rumble of a man's, but not the light young voice of Dougal that she had come to know, as he so often

called in on Mary. This was a rough, abrupt, authorita-
tive voice that she could not remember having heard
before, but for some reason it fell over her bright morning
and her new feeling of safety like a pall of darkness which
she could not understand. She could hear the other children in their piping voices being careful of their manners
and not behaving with the loving familiarity that was
their custom with the queen, and when Mary brought
her bowl of porridge and her piece of rough meal bread,
she did not stay with her but bade her to try carefully
and manage by herself this morning, and not to drop any
of the porridge on her shift. Merca's reasonless fear would
not let her eat, and the bowl of porridge was still full and
cooled between her fingers when she heard Queen Margaret speak beyond the curtain of her doorway.

"We have another one in here," she said, and her voice
was full of sad reproach, "getting better from starvation,
and I cannot begin to tell you, Malcolm, how it grieves
me to think where she has come from." But she did not
tell him at that moment, and as her gold-ringed hand
swept back the door curtain and the wooden rings rat-
tled on their pole, the name she had uttered blazed as if
engraved in scarlet before Merca's eyes, hazing into a
mist of hate and terror so that the porridge tipped from
her nerveless fingers, falling in a cold congealing lump
into the white softness of the sheepskin.

Malcolm! Malcolm, King of Scotia. How could she not
have thought? Where there was a queen there was always
a king, and since she had seen them together in Wearmouth, why had it not occurred to her that they might

93

have married each other, turning her princess into a queen—queen of the country in which they had been wandering. Starvation had stolen away her wits, but now they were coming back in such a torrent of disappointment and fury and hatred that she hardly saw the genial red-bearded face that came no further than the door, nor heard the anxious cry of the queen who took one look at her stiff white face and left at once, calling urgently for Mary. The hate and fury were now not only for the king, but for the queen who had so bitterly disappointed her by being his wife.

ong before the bell boomed into the following dawn, Merca was awake and her plans laid. Throughout the previous day she had puzzled and distressed Mary with her stony face, and with her cold refusal to take any food or to answer anything that she was asked. She steeled herself against their kindness and against the good steaming food by reminding herself that they were all provided by her hated enemy, to whom she would not be beholden even while she planned to take his life. Now in the cold dark before the faint light had begun to thin the blackness beyond her window, she threw back the warm friendship of the piled skins and crept across the cold rushes to the bed on the other side of the room where Dag was still asleep.

They must leave at once. It did not matter where they went, but they could not stay here in the palace of this monster. She could care for Dag, without the charity of this black-hearted man who had burnt their home, killed their parents, and sold them into slavery. Nor did she want anything now from the queen, who must be as evil as he, however she might seem, else why would she be his wife? Firmly she thrust away the thought of the fair, gentle face and the kind hands that had so tenderly soothed her grief. She and Dag could manage on their own. Already, in the dark mist of hate that had closed across her mind, she had forgotten that it was but a few short days since she had been close to death from hunger, and Dag with her, in her efforts to care for them both.

Her weak legs startled her a little as she stumbled across the floor, and put the first thin thread of doubt through the fury of her resolve, but she stiffened her knees determinedly and told herself that it would pass.

"Dag," she whispered, crouching beside the low bed where he lay in a warm tangle with his small bed mate. "Dag!" she whispered fiercely again, and he stirred, rumpling the straw so that it tickled her face as she bent over him and she clapped her hands over her nose in her efforts not to sneeze; but Dag had not wakened. Desperately she reached out and shook him, terrified of waking the other child, and at last he opened his eyes, dark, sleepy eyes in the dead light that was growing just sufficiently to show them to each other as paler shadows.

"Dag, we must go away. Quickly now get up, and we will be gone before light."

Even though he did not move, it was as if Dag tensed himself there in his warm bed. He did not answer her, but lay quite still and looked at her as if he had not understood.

"We have got to run away," she hissed again, underlining every word. "This is the palace of the King of Scotia, did you not know that? We cannot stay here."

Dag knew whose palace it was, and it meant nothing to him any more.

"I know whose palace it is," he said. "I have known for days."

"Well!" In the gray shadows, Merca looked at him in amazement, wondering what he was waiting for and why he did not jump up at once. "We cannot stay here!"

The little boy searched desperately around for some way out. He was firm and clear in his own thoughts, but when Merca was like this he was a little afraid of her, and it took all his courage to face what he must do. He looked at her pale shape, peering at him with furious eyes in the growing light.

"You have no clothes," he said firmly. "I have, but you haven't, sister, and you would get cold."

Merca was growing frantic. At any moment one of the other children might stir and wake, crying out so as to bring Mary from the curtained bed in the far corner, or the bell might begin its calling for the first Office and then all the queen's household would be astir, and the chance gone. Irritably she plucked at the creamy woolen robe she had been wearing in bed.

"I have more clothes," she hissed, "than I have had on my back for more than a year since. Dag, I beg you *come*. We must go at *once!*"

She got up, ready to lead and for Dag to follow as always, but Dag's long amiable mouth folded suddenly into a tight line, and his wide gray eyes narrowed a little.

"No," he said, and said no more, but it brought her wheeling on him in fury.

"You must, you must, you must!" she cried hoarsely, forgetting to whisper. "We cannot stay here and live in this man's house! He is your enemy, Dag! But for him you would have your father and your mother and your home!" She was almost sobbing in her anger, but some sudden caution with this new Dag made her hold back from telling him of her plans. Why had Dag no *spirit?*

97

Dag did not lack spirit, but he was very young and he lacked a long memory. His father and mother and his home had long since faded to no more than the occasional sharp recollection that he did not properly understand. Much more real to him now were the kind faces around him and the good meals on the table and the pictures in the queen's book, and the soft-spoken monks who had promised him that he himself should write. Slowly he sat up and fumbled in the corner of the straw where he had hidden his shell, his face growing calmer as his nervous fingers found the loved curves. He looked full and steady at his sister, clear now beside him in her pale, full-skirted gown with her blue eyes black with anger, the light of dawn on her fierce white face. Apologetically, as was his way, he leaned over and planted a kiss on her cheek.

"No," he said again and looked at her worriedly; and helpless, she knew he meant it, however difficult it had been for him to say. Even as they faced each other in hopeless disagreement, the bell began its slow steady call for Matins and the glow of candlelight sprang warm behind the scattered windows; the Palace of Dunfermline awoke to the day's life.

By the time the queen swept in among her laughing, clinging children for the morning meal, Merca had come to terms with her situation. Helpless and furious she had left the silent Dag and crept back to her bed to glare at him in raging frustration, gnawing at her nails while her mind rushed here and there trying to decide for both of them what she should do. She had been looking after Dag for so long that it did not occur to her that this time it might be different; that Dag had already made his decision and it might not be the same as her own. After a while she grew calmer, and thought that perhaps Dag's obstinacy might suit her well. It was foolish to have been in such a hurry to run away, for she could hate Malcolm just as fiercely close to him as she could at a distance, and would it not itself be a sweet vengeance to be living in his household while she sought the gold to have him killed? When she had raised the gold, it would be easier to summon Thomas to the home of the king himself, than to seek him if she herself was a wanderer. She began to smile, a cold little smile that would have frightened Dag. She had now come to think that everything was being made easy for her, and it would have been madness to run away.

To kill a king! Both she and Thomas of the Knife longed for the same end, but for her part she might wait in comfort, eating the king's food and living in his dwelling, until the moment came. She had some anxiety as to how she was going to get this gold, but soon dismissed it. All things were shaping in her favor, and that would surely come easily too, if she but waited.

The queen was different. Merca had already fallen spell to her sweet gentleness and her beauty, but she told herself grimly that she must learn to hate Margaret, too, for how could she be what she seemed, and yet be content wedded to the monster King of Scotia. So the queen who came smiling to her bedside with the small ones clinging to her bright skirts was puzzled and distressed to find a girl who answered her questions with few words and cold and stony eyes and would speak no more.

"Mary, what ails her?" the queen asked as she went out, baffled by the sharp, unhappy face that had in these last few days begun to show traces of prettiness again. "Something is wrong since yesterday." The queen's face was full of distress. "Mary, she looks at us suddenly as if she hates us. What have we done?"

Mary shrugged, as puzzled as her mistress.

"I have no notion, Madam. I asked the little brother, but he looked at me sideways from those great big eyes of his, and would say nothing."

They both smiled then, for there were few who could think of the small abstracted, elderly Dag without a smile.

"She will be happier," the queen said hopefully, "now that she is well enough to leave her bed and know a little freedom." She faced out across the paved courtyard that was warm with the first real sun of summer, and soft with the cooing of the strutting pigeons, and her thoughts flew ahead of her feet to her own baby son whom she would visit next. He was her first born son, hers and Malcolm's; her beloved rough, savage Malcolm, whose heart had been rooted in war and battle, and who had known no music but the clang of weapons all his life, and thought soft words and manners to be made only for the use of fools and women. Merca could never have believed or understood the tender smile on the queen's mouth as she thought of him. She loved him because, in all his roughness, he was gentle to her in all things, and had made valiant attempts for her sake to turn his thoughts from endless war; even to shape himself clumsily to her quiet ways and generous life. He looked with wonder at his gay and lovely wife who was concerned only with the giving of life, to the poor and the hungry, the orphaned and the sick, asking nothing for herself.

So it was that the Court of Dunfermline around which Merca began to move in the summer of 1071, was a place of peace and happiness, for all its roughness, and was beginning to echo the sweet contentment of Malcolm and Margaret in their young marriage and their baby son. Only in the blue hate-shadowed eyes of Merca did Malcolm appear as an unforgiven and unforgivable murderer, and his wife as one who must be no better since she had married him. But Merca's hatred could not blind her completely to all the pleasures and interests of her new life, and gradually she grew familiar with the people who made up the household, watching them at mealtimes from her lowly table. As she was the eldest of all the adopted children, she did not live apart entirely as did the little ones; she slept with them as from the start, but had her meals in the common hall, sitting at the lowest of the women's tables and at right angles to all the rest. The first time she came in she looked with curiosity around the vast smoke-blackened room. It was decorated on its timber walls only by crossed weapons and caps of steel and great round shields with heavy bosses, all dulled with smoke and steam and soot. The trestle tables were stained deep with grease and scored with knife cuts, and the hearth fire blazed in the center of the floor, hazing the whole great chamber with its reeking turf smoke, and lifting more layers of soot from burning logs to clog the dripping roof beams. The only thing of beauty was the long carved double seat along the middle of the side table where Malcolm sat with his queen. Without being able to put thought into words, Merca knew it for a room where only men who did not care much for their surroundings had lived.

She did not look much at the king and queen, for she knew all she wanted to of them, but she watched the dark, impatient ways of the queen's sister, the Princess Christina, who had not wanted to wait that day at Wearmouth, and sensed that in some way she did not like the king. She was terrified of Queen Margaret's mother, who was large and awkward and noisy, always talking in a muddled way and shouting everybody down, even the king. She looked with caution and a little pity at Malcolm's young fair-haired son, Duncan. She was sorry for him because Mary had told her that he was the son of the king's first wife who was dead, and so, like her, he had no mother. But she was cautious too, for Duncan was a wild one, always up to pranks and never to be trusted.

It was a rough and savage court, not yet much influenced by the queen's gentleness. She had been there little beyond a year, but even as she was taming the warlike Malcolm, so she thought of taming his household.

On Merca's third evening in the hall, she sat devouring the good plentiful food provided by the king she planned to kill, gathering her strength so that she might turn her mind to gathering gold. The meal was ending—the tables running with the blood of half-cooked meats, and scarred with the day's fresh knife cuts—the warm air was hazy with the smell of smoke and cooling fat. Bread was broken and crumbled all along the trenchers and the wine cups were empty. As was their custom, the first to finish were lurching to their feet, stepping out between their companions and the benches, belching their pleasure in their dinner, and wiping their mouths along their greasy sleeves. Merca sensed a movement at the middle table and peered through the smoke to see the queen whispering urgently to the king. Malcolm shrugged his heavy shoulders and looked doubtful. However, he leapt at once to his feet in answer to the queen's request and hammered on the table with the haft of his own grease-crusted dagger.

"My lords!" he cried, and arrested them as they moved, their legs across the benches. "My lords and gentlemen! The Queen has received a cargo of fair wine from France. She asks you to honor her by taking a cup with her when the meal is ended. It will be passed around when grace is said."

Astonished and open-mouthed they subsided again onto their benches and looked at each other, realizing what they had done, or rather what the queen had so graciously done for them. She had compelled them to remain at table until the grace was said, and for the first time in Malcolm's hall, the black-robed monk stood up to say the evening grace and did not have to say it to empty benches, or to the last few indifferent laggards arguing over their cold mouthfuls on some point of war.

"Benedictus, benedicat. Bless us and bless what we have eaten."

Grace fell into an astonished silence, and then the

stewards flew with the fresh wine ready for the queen's tasting, and with trays of sweetmeats, new and strange on these rough tables, so that when Queen Margaret rose and smiled at them, lifted her jeweled goblet, and thanked them for sharing her wine with her, they rose to a man and remained standing, almost bemused, until she and a smiling Malcolm had left the hall.

"Well, well, well!" An old lady spoke across Merca's head as they in their turn went out. "I have been here since the boy Duncan was a child, nor have I ever seen that pack of men more sweetly brought to heel. And she will do it every night, until she teaches them proper manners, whether they will or no."

Another woman laughed.

"They have never dallied a moment when their stomachs were full to get even the Lord's blessing. Well, tonight they got it and the Queen's blessing as well."

"The Queen's blessing," the first woman echoed approvingly. "It is the name for it."

"The Queen's blessing!"

For one moment Merca listened, wishing that the blessing from the smiling queen might have been for her too, and that she did not have to hate. It was like a moment's light in a cold darkness that closed down again immediately. She wanted no blessings, but to live here for one purpose only. The brief sadness vanished, and her mouth tightened in a face that reflected the cold hardness of her hatred.

It troubled her that Dag would not hate, for she and Dag were one, but to all her urgings Dag turned his bland face and dark watchful eyes. Then he would smile his slow smile and tell her of something he had done in the small timber monastery down the steep hill where he spent all his days, or of something he had seen in the deep glen that flowered now with the Scottish summer. If she pressed him, he would fish in the new pouch for his shell and his nervous fingers around the curves would show his anxiety, but he would not be shaken. Dag was happy. He could not find words to say so, but he was traitor to all her hating, loving his new life and the good people who had given it to him, and determined to give up nothing for old wounds he could now barely remember.

So she had to hate for both of them, in the clear northern sunshine, learning her way around the Palace of Dunfermline; a simple place as yet, no more than a clutter of buildings at the very lip of the glen; a mass of timber and wattle halls and bowers, roofed with heavy thatch and clustered around courts that hazed with dust in summer and ran with mud in winter. On the highest spur above the glen, Malcolm was building himself a fine stone fortress because, for the first time, he was stricken with the fears that he and his men had brought without thought into countless homes, including Merca's own. He had his queen now, and his baby son; and cold fear possessed him that in his absence some enemy might attack, and his loved ones would be as helpless as any peasants in their blazing wattle home.

The stone walls of the tower were rising square and pale and uncompromising against the summer sky, but farther down the hill they were digging the foundations of another building, more dear to Queen Margaret's heart—the Church of the Holy Trinity, beside the little timber structure where she and the king were married. There was little to be seen as yet, save the raw shape of the trenches in the peaty soil and the first cargos of fresh stone, swinging from the wagons on the tall pillars of wooden tackle, ready to be shaped lovingly by the Saxon stonemasons who had followed their princess from England. Here Merca loved to come and watch when she could steal away alone, listening to the broad Saxon vowels and feeling a little less alone, but always wondering how these Saxons could settle so happily in the strange northern court.

The noon bell caught her loitering there one day when she should have been helping the lady Mary and those others who, under the supervision of the queen, fed the multitudes of the poor each day at noon. Today, Queen Margaret was not in Dunfermline, nor was the king, both having ridden away on the previous day, and life in the palace was not quite as strict and orderly as usual. Mary, missing the child, and troubled always by her closed unhappy face, had let her be and sent no one to look for her. As Merca came rushing through the door of the monastery refectory on the last stroke of the bell, she was full of anxious apology, for now that her course was clear she was very careful not to do anything that might cause displeasure or lead to her being sent away.

"My lady Mary, forgive me. I forgot."

"It is no matter. Take the basket now and see to the bread as you know how."

The poor came in silence, shuffling dumbly across the floor with the drag of their feet only overlaid by the droning murmur of the noon Office sung by the monks in the chapel next door; all except those who supervised in the refectory, the duty of charity being so holy in the eyes of their order that their rule excused them even their Office. Merca knew exactly how much bread she should give to each hungry creature, but her own hunger was too recent in her mind for her to be careful, and her basket was always empty long before she had reached the end of her allotted tables, sending her to stand apologetically before the buttery door, sniffing at the strange mixed smell of herbs and meat and fresh-baked bread, and the tangy odor of home-brewed ale.

"More so soon?" The rosy, friendly face of the monk in the buttery would look out at her and he would shake his head. "They are hungry, these ones that you feed!" But he would give her more, unconcerned about the cost, for it was the queen's charity, and where the poor were concerned the royal coffers did not seem to have a bottom.

This was one of the rare places where Merca would smile back happily, for like Dag, she felt secure in the presence of these serene and cheerful men with their odd round haircuts and their great hoods hooked like ears below their chins. Today she did not have time to speak, for as she reached the buttery door for the second time there was a clatter of hoofs and a commotion in the yard outside, and in a moment the queen stood in the open door, the sunlight staining her green gown to yellow and lighting her hair with threads of gold. Usually she moved among her poor, who lifted their grateful faces as she spoke with them and urged them to eat, and to tell her of their troubles. Today she neither smiled nor spoke, but stood there in the flood of golden sunshine looking at them with an expression on her face almost of fear, as if they were some task too great for her, her thin hands clasping and unclasping round the tassels of her girdle.

"All of them," she said at last, aloud, but as if to herself. "All of them, within my whole kingdom. It is a monstrous task, but before Heaven I will not shrink from it, so long as I can find the gold. Malcolm must give it to me!"

Merca started and dropped a piece of bread in the rushes. As she bent to pick it up she was astonished to think that she and the queen should both be seeking gold. What might the queen need it for?

The queen turned abruptly and left, in a whirl of grass-green skirts, and Mary moved over quickly to her brother, who had come in behind Queen Margaret.

"What ails her, Dougal? She is pale and not herself. Where have you been with them?"

Dougal shook a puzzled head, his long curling hair as black and shining as his sister's.

"I know and yet I don't know. We have escorted them to a place on Loch Leven where a company of holy men live solitary upon an island, and it seems the queen begged the abbot there to allow her to make some gift to him and his community. He refused all things that she could give him, but charged her to take on her shoulders the care of all the poor and homeless in the entire kingdom of Scotia, bidding her to make them her especial business. She is much disturbed, feeling for some reason that this a command of God, but I think it is honest housekeeping now that troubles her, for it is a big task and will take a fair deal of gold."

Mary's bright face grew soft with affection.

"She takes every smallest thing in her life, Dougal, as the command of God, but do not fret. If it is for the good of someone else, then she will find the gold."

Merca was still listening, her basket of bread forgotten on her arm, and her face grew hard and thoughtful. It was one thing to give bread over generously to the poor at the queen's expense, but gold was another matter. She herself had an urgent need for gold, and she wondered how the queen could come by it so easily.

o project in all Scotia was closer at this moment to the queen's heart than the building of the Church of the Holy Trinity. Day after day she spent contented hours pouring over plans and drawings with her architects and Saxon stonemasons, determined that this church should be the loveliest thing that this country of Scotia had ever raised to the glory of God. Because it was the interest of his Margaret, Malcolm struggled gallantly to take his mind from his bleak tower and set aside his usual way of thinking in terms of arrow slits and bastions, in order to brood with her over plans for soaring roof and arches of flowing stone. She was anxious that by the time the church was built, all the rich altar cloths and vestments needed for its furnishing should be ready, and she called around her the most skilled needlewomen of the court, to work daily in her bower over the fine silks and splendid satins close-stitched with gold and silver and scarlet and green that would bring splendor and warmth to the cold gray shell of the new church.

"And have you ever used your needle, daughter?" she asked Merca one morning as she visited her children, struggling as always to find something that might warm life and interest in this child's cold, unfriendly face. And for one moment, Merca's hard expression trembled, brought suddenly back to the memory of a piece of pricked and draggled cloth and her mother's patient fingers guiding her small hand with the needle.

"A long time since, madam," she answered, herself again, "and I have forgotten."

"Well," the queen said, trying to kindle her interest, "we will see how nimble those fingers might be if we teach you afresh."

"I could hold a needle." The clear, self-satisfied voice spoke from beside her where Dag, untouched by his sister's coldness, leaned amiably against the queen's arm, nodding his head a little in his interest. Queen Margaret smiled down at the grave face, and Merca looked at him and could almost include him in her dark hatred because he looked so contented. He had no *right* to look happy here in this place. She felt suddenly bewildered, as if she had forgotten why she must go on with all this lonely hating, while Dag leaned happily on the crimson of the queen's sleeve and rubbed an appreciative finger up and down the fringes of her cuff. "I could hold a needle I am sure," he said again, "for the Father says I am a genius with the pen." He looked gravely and impressively up at the queen, slightly affronted when she broke into a help-less laugh, stroking his round cheek.

"Then that is excellent, little son," she said when she could stop. "You will busy yourself with your so clever pen, and we will teach your sister to hold the needle."

His sister would have died before she admitted how much pleasure it gave her when she was allowed to join the needlewomen. Although at first her efforts were poor and clumsy and she often spattered her small piece of cloth with the blood of her pricked fingers, she learned quickly. Her hands were neat and careful, earning even the grudging praise of the ill-tempered Princess Christina, whose impatient fingers flew miraculously over the most exquisite embroidery in the palace.

"When I was a young girl little older than you," the princess said to Merca, nodding her dark head proudly over her lovely work, "I was allowed to embroider an altar cloth for the great Minister of St. Peter, that our dear lord the Confessor built in London."

The queen's hands came to rest on her embroidery frame, and her eyes were soft and distant on something she alone could see.

"Among the apple orchards, he built it," she said softly, and smiled as if she had loved the place. "On the edge of the marshes at Westminster, where the kingcups grew along the Thames." It was only a few of her watching ladies who knew that it was among these kingcups in a London spring that she had first met Malcolm, but Merca saw only her exquisitely serene and happy face and knew a moment of desperate longing to love her as everybody else did; everyone striving in her presence to be a little better than they were.

She took her mind off the queen by looking around her bower where Merca had never been before; a big square chamber with wattle walls ill-covered by a few hanging curtains that did nothing to keep out the drafts. There was a vast carved bed that looked like a boat brought in from the shore and filled with straw and down. It was heaped with furs and woolen covers and bright-colored pillows, and there was little else save a few rough shelves along a wall, two carved chests for clothes, and the kneeling bench where she spent so much time at prayer. Her psalter was open on it to the brilliant pages that so fascinated Dag, and beside it on a table stood a carved and jeweled chest that was the only other thing of beauty in the room, curiously wrought, with gold and silver gleaming in the locks. It was simple quarters for a queen, and was still marked with the rough hand of Malcolm who had done his loving best, but Margaret had not yet had time to lay over the whole palace the clear mark of her own exquisite taste and love of beauty.

As the word of her bounty and charity spread through the kingdom, the numbers of the poor who came to be fed grew daily larger and larger, presenting themselves in their hundreds at the refectory door at noon, and now Merca learnt to be careful with her bread for not even the tolerant buttery monk could provide her with more when her baskets were empty. By chance, she stood one day behind the queen as she left the refectory with Mary, her fair face creased with distress as she looked at the long silent line who still waited outside to be fed.

"I am troubled, Mary, over the cost of all this, even though it be God's work."

Mary looked as anxious as she.

"The money that the king has granted us, madam, is not enough now the numbers grow so large."

"I know, I know. And I am loath to trouble the king for more." Her anxious face melted into a tender and affectionate smile. "For so much of his life, he knew nothing of charity, so that he does not now part easily with gold for it. He would more willingly equip a company with chain mail! But we will teach him, dear Mary. We will teach him."

When the queen left, Merca followed her as soon as she was able. In the morning when they had all sat at needlework, the Princess Christina, with one of her blunt careless kindnesses, had given her a few ends of silk and she had kept them for Dag, thinking how he would get pleasure from the bright rose and apricot sheen of the silk in the sun. The noon bell had caught them unawares, absorbed in their work, and there had been a great hurrying during which the bright silks had slipped forgotten to the rushes. Now Merca crept back to ask the queen if she might look for them, set on giving Dag this small pleasure.

The hall was empty on this high summer day, everybody was out about the palace on their many duties, and through the vast room the shafts of sunlight fell on the drying rushes and turned the glowing hearth fire to a heap of dead white ash. Somewhere a man was singing one of the strange Gaelic songs, all of people dying, and from the solar beyond the hall Merca could hear the voice of the Princess Agatha raised in her loud, perpetual complaint. The door to the queen's bower stood open and the curtain was looped back against the heat of the still day, and as Merca reached the opening she was about to beg the pardon of the queen, whom she could see inside, when something halted her. Queen Margaret stood in the middle of the room and quite alone, but her face looked all at once guilty and mischievous, like a child knowing it is going to do some fairly harmless wrong, and she bubbled with helpless laughter. For a moment she glanced around to be sure she was alone, never noticing the girl in the doorway, and then she moved over and lifted the lid of the jeweled casket on the table.

Merca's hand flew to her mouth to silence her astonished gasp. The queen had plunged her hands into the small chest and brought them out dripping with gold coins which she packed into the pouch at her waist, her face filled all the while with this same strange mixture of mischief and guilt. Another fistful and Merca held her breath not to cry out, but there was someone else to cry out before her.

"Thief! I have you, thief! Caught in the very moment!"

The curtain across the other door was swept aside and Malcolm strode across the room to grasp the queen's dripping fistful in his huge hairy hand, grinning down into her appalled face.

"Oh, Malcolm—I—"

Merca waited for no more, uncertain whether the queen laughed or wept and unable to understand any of it. She shot back into the hall and hid behind a stack of trestles, for she could hear them already coming out, and then see them, the king leading the queen by the hand he still held full of the gold, and shouting down her protests, crying that she could deny nothing when he had caught her in the act.

"Page!" he bellowed at the top of his mighty voice, and Merca waited in sick cold horror for the clash of men at arms, distressed to be present at such a moment, her hatred forgotten. She could not understand though, why there was this grin on the king's face when he had caught his queen red-handed as a thief, nor the way she stood and bit her lip with bright laughing eyes as though it was a game she must submit to. "Page!" he shouted again, even as the startled boy ran in. "Go get me Father Turgot! Get me the queen's confessor! I care not if he is at his prayers, tell him the Queen has need to tell her sins!"

The boy's eyes were as big as saucers as he shot away, and no more surprised than those of the dark-haired monk who came in a few moments later, though his face held to its normal studied calm, his pace even and his hands quiet in his black sleeves. Only his lively and curious eyes betrayed that there was anything unusual in his summons.

"The Queen!" cried Malcolm, and now he could not control his gusty laughter that rang to the sooty beams. "The Queen, good Father Turgot, wishes to confess herself a thief!"

The calm pale face only echoed Malcolm's laughter with a smile that was full of the affection which everybody bore the queen, knowing now that the situation was not serious.

"And what has our lady Queen stolen?" he asked.

Malcolm held her captive hand above the table.

"Open!" he bellowed. "Open!"

The handful of small gold coins poured onto the table, tumbling darker gold into a clear patch of sun. From her hiding place, Merca peered out in complete open-mouthed bewilderment, utterly unable to understand the gentle, tolerant face of the priest or Malcolm's delighted grin and the helpless laughter of the queen. A couple of the little coins rolled off the table into the rushes and Malcolm dived after them.

"My special gold," he cried, clutching them. "My coins so specially minted for the offerings at your Masses, good Father Turgot, and for my Maundy money for the poor. Oh yes, even I know that there are poor in Scotia! And I find this wicked thief plundering my casket. What her punishment, Father, and what her penance?"

Even as he thundered his accusations, his big rugged, red-whiskered face was soft with tenderness, and he put an arm around his thief, who laid her head against his shoulder, smiling ruefully at the priest.

"Oh, my lord and king," she said, and her laughter still bubbled. "I had not sufficient gold to feed my people, and dared not ask your angry face for more. So I went looking for it where I well knew I would find it."

In behind the shadow of her trestles, Merca sat back on her heels, rocked again by this feeling of bewilderment, uncertain for a second as to why she must be shadowed by black hate in a place where the whole atmosphere seemed soft with kindness and love; where it was almost impossible to remember that this big teasing red-haired man was the monster of cruelty she had vowed to kill; where even the aloof and quiet priest looked at the queen with a gentleness and affection that was almost the equal of Malcolm's own.

"Her penance," Malcolm cried again. "Her penance, my Father," and the priest smiled.

"Only let the Queen not waste the gold," he said. "Nor

will she, for feeding the hungry is an instruction of Our Lord Himself, and there are many more in need of her help."

The queen sighed then and her laughing face grew shadowed, as if all the poor and suffering of her husband's kingdom weighed against her heart. Slowly she gathered up the spilt coins and heaped them back into her pouch.

"I thank my lord for his gift," she said, and once more the mischief touched her face. "And I promise the Father Turgot that I will not waste it."

"Gift!" roared Malcolm. "Gift!" He would have started again, but with a small bend of her head towards the priest, the queen had withdrawn into her bower, and there in a few moments the king followed her.

When the sandals of the monk had fallen silent in the dust beyond the door, and the hall was left again to the drifting sunlight and one ragged hound nosing for scraps among the rushes, Merca came slowly from her hiding place, her face sharply lined with thought. She could not make head or tail of the scene she had just watched, but only understood that the queen had stolen the king's gold, and no one had done anything but laugh, even the monk. Could it be as easy as this to come by gold? All the gold she wanted? If the queen could steal, surely it was not wrong for her either, and the king would only laugh to lose his gold. Or would he? Dimly she felt there was something in the situation that was beyond her. The gold itself was certainly within her reach and as soon as she was not face to face with gentleness and laughter, it was very easy to remember cold and hunger and homelessness; easy to be as fierce as ever for vengeance on the man who had brought all these things upon herself and Dag. But the thought of Dag jolted her. He was serene and stolid once again, with his round, serious face content and the straight fall of his fair hair shining, looking at her with obstinate and determined disinterest when she tried to talk of hate. Quickly she put the thought from her mind. She and Dag were one, as they had always been, and she knew what was best for Dag and would look after him. The first step in her plans lay here beside her hand, close and easy. As she stepped out of the hall into the sunlight of the courtyard her face was deliberately calm and she smoothed the skirts of her blue woolen kirtle as if the gesture smoothed the excitement from her eyes lest anyone might mark it.

t was some while before Merca got another chance to go alone into the queen's
bower. There were long days of heavy
rain that brought the clouds from the mountains to hang
in the very tree tops of the glen and obscure all sight of
the distant sea. The court was confined within the halls
and bowers, dank smelling from the rain-soaked wattle,
and cold and clammy under their weight of dripping
thatch. With the return of the sun, the ladies all trooped
gratefully out behind the queen into the damp, steaming
world that glittered with the crystals of the rain. Behind
them came the servants with chairs and bolsters and
embroidery frames, setting them up on the grass below
the tower in the welcome sunshine. The company could
look down along the damp thickets of the trees, under
which pink drifts of willow herb and the tall spikes of fox-
glove patched the wild undergrowth of the glen. Queen
Margaret settled herself in her carved chair and smiled at
her ladies.

"I feel myself taken from prison today," she said, looking gratefully over the moist green world, with the piles of
stone for the new church still patched black with damp
and the swollen ropes screeching in the windlasses.
"There is nothing more difficult than to be closed within
during the precious days of summer."

The Princess Agatha made some loud scathing remark
about the rigors of a Scottish summer being more tiresome
than winter in any Christian land. Merca scarcely heard

it. She was looking coldly at the queen and remembering the days of her and Dag's captivity; asking herself what this beautiful highborn lady in her brilliant gown could ever know about being closed in against her will. Now that she was able to see her way clear to what she wanted to do, she found it easier to think of nothing else, and her relentless hatred was less often undermined by those sudden treacherous doubts which she did not understand.

"Merca! My child! What dream are you in? And what an unhappy dream it must be so to furrow your face and darken your eyes! Do you not hear me?"

Merca started so that the point of the needle shot into her finger and in an instant the blood beaded the bright silk under her hand. She heard the Princess Christina cluck with anger, but Queen Margaret silenced her with a small gesture.

"You were very far away from us." She looked with concern at the child, whose face was always clouded by some unhappiness that she could not penetrate. For the thousandth time she sighed and shivered in sudden misery at the ravages of the wars so dear to her husband's heart —wars that left young children like this girl with shadowed faces and dark minds that no love could reach. It comforted her a little that since their marriage, her fierce husband had hung up his sword, and she prayed daily that this might be forever so, and that Malcolm would find other ways of settling the disputes of Scotia with her Norman neighbors. She brought her mind back to Merca, anguish over all her husband's wars narrowing to pity for this young victim of them, and she cast about for something to break the girl away from whatever she was thinking of, and to ease the look of strain from her face.

"Merca, I have an errand I would ask you to do." She held up a skein of silk, yellow as marigolds in the sunlight, pushing the others out of sight in the folds of her skirts. "I have too little of this silk for what I would do. Will you go for me to my bower? The silks are all there as you know, folded into their covers on the shelves. Will you match this for me?"

"I will go for you, madam, and be sure to get the right one."

Mary was already on her feet, but the queen waved her back to her blue bolster on the grass.

"Let her go, dear Mary, let her go." She watched the stiff back of Merca as she walked away, its rigid unfriend-liness not hidden by the swing of her saffron skirt. For the sake of all such children she must redouble her prayers that Malcolm might have hung up his sword forever.

Merca had come alone into the hall many times, and since her mind was free from guilt in what she did, she had taken small notice of the man-at-arms on guard out-side the door, nor had he paid any attention to her. Today, as she picked her way between the muddy patches that still oozed wet with rain, she was torn with doubt about what she was going to do, but filled with the certainty that she *must* do it. It was particularly sweet vengeance that she should steal gold to pay for the king's death from the king himself, and when it was done, she thought exultantly, then she and Dag would be free once more.

She had hated so long and blindly that she could not see that she and Dag were as free and safe as they had ever been, even in their own home. But even if killing gave her no thought but fierce pleasure, she could not shed the feeling that it was wrong to steal; so as she passed the guard her eyes were shifty, and she edged in through the door, not looking at him.

The guard was a married man with children of his own down beyond the glen, in the clustered huts of Malcolm's married soldiers, and he looked after the edging, furtive child with an experienced eye. There, he thought, is someone up to mischief, and turned his head away, watching from the corners of his eyes to see what she might be going to do. He was a little surprised to hear her scuff steadily across the hall, and leaped sharply inside the door at the rattle of the heavy curtain rings of the queen's bower, just in time to see Merca vanishing inside it. Astonished, he moved quickly after her, and reached the door of the bower as she took her first glittering fistful from the casket.

"By my soul," he roared then. "This is no prank! Come, thief, and face the Queen, and then likely the hangman. What viper is she raising!"

Even as he grabbed her by the neck as he might grab a puppy and shook the coins from her hand, Merca knew with cold, sudden terror that the king would not laugh. She was caught, and the king would not laugh. Limp with fright, she made no attempt to struggle, and her only thought was for Dag. She had made a mess of this, and now what was Dag to do; Dag who could not live alone!

When they reached the queen, she felt numb and faint with fear as she listened to the soldier pouring out his tale and saw, as if at a great distance, the horror on the queen's face as she got to her feet, the gay silks falling in a cascade to the ground. Some corner of Merca's mind noticed that she had several more skeins of the color she had sent her for, and she tried to reason why, but her dark, frightened eyes were on Queen Margaret's face. The instinct to fight that had brought her and Dag through so many terrible days was gradually bubbling up through her terror.

"Merca," said the queen, and her voice was little more than a whisper. "Oh, Merca, and we have given you everything."

Her face was not angry but astonished and distressed, and Merca sensed the same reproach and amazement on the faces of all the ladies round her. She felt herself the center of a ring of self-righteous and bewildered eyes, and the fingers of the man-at-arms were hard and painful on the back of her neck. With a fierce gesture she wriggled herself free and stamped before the queen, her head high, and her blue eyes blazing, fear forgotten.

"You did it!" she cried. "You did it!" All respect abandoned, she glared with furious satisfaction at the queen's shattered face. "I saw you, madam, stealing the King's gold just as I tried to do, and he only laughed and so did Father Turgot, and no one was angry. If you can steal from the king, then why cannot I?"

The queen collapsed back into her chair as if she had taken a spear between the shoulders.

"You saw—the day I took the gold?" she asked faintly, and all her ladies stared wide-eyed from her to the triumphant child and back again, longing to ask what it was all about.

"I saw, madam," Merca said, and added again. "If it is not wrong for you to steal, then why is it wrong for me?"

"Where were you?"

"Behind the piled trestles in a corner of the Hall."

The queen shook her head in silence, as if she was gathering time to know how to deal with this, and from about her feet Mary gathered up the pale silks of festival which she had been embroidering, and smoothed them in her lap.

"You may go," Queen Margaret said then to the guard. "Yes, leave her to me. You may go," she added sharply at his obvious reluctance, and slowly he left, muttering about justice in his beard, for he was a Scot and had his own views already about the number of penniless Saxons that cluttered the court of the King of Scotia. His bare red shanks moved off slowly down the hill. The queen turned to Merca, who was a little disconcerted to see no anger or condemnation, only gentleness and pity.

"What did you want it for, little daughter?" she asked, and Merca blinked, for before that sweet, understanding face, the reason seemed suddenly impossible and silly.

"To care for Dag," she said, and in a way it was true, for she did not want to add lying to stealing.

The queen shook her head in puzzlement, pushing back the soft edges of her veil as if to see Merca more clearly that she might understand her.

"But we will care for Dag," she said. "Do you not trust us?"

Merca was silent, unable to answer this, and the queen reached out a hand and drew her close, feeling the stiff resentment of the young body and grieving for it. Oh, my dear Malcolm, she thought. You and your beloved fighting. As well as those you have killed, how many more children have you left like this?

"We will care for Dag," she said again to the girl, and watched hopefully for any sign of softening in the unyielding face. "And we will care for you too—always. There is no need to steal, for we will give you all you need." She smiled a little. "And you could not have used the King's gold, for it is marked most specially as his."

Still Merca did not answer, for she had nothing to say.

"And you will learn some day," the queen added, and now her smile grew full and warm, but it was not for Merca. "You will learn some day that if you are blessed by God with a happy marriage, then your husband is glad to share all he has with you, and there can be no stealing one from the other, no matter what may be said in jest."

The girl's interest was caught and she lifted a puzzled face.

"You mean you were really taking what belonged to you, too?"

Again the queen smiled.

"Yes, so of course he could not have been truly angry."

"Well then, why did he make such an uproar and call in the good Father?" Catching Mary's reproving gaze,

Merca knew that in her need to understand, she had forgotten all politeness and respect, but the queen did not appear to mind. She only shrugged and laughed again and her face glowed with some secret happiness, brighter than all the spangled raindrops on the flowers.

"He jested," she said. "He only jested, to tease me. Now, my child, go down to the church and ask God to forgive you for what you have tried to do. I myself forgive you freely, for I do not think it is you who are to blame."

This also Merca did not quite understand, but obediently she went down the rain-scored hillside to the church, where she found she was glad to be alone. She sat on one of the rough benches in the cool shadows with the sun pouring warm through a window onto her folded hands, and the blackbirds whistling in the trees outside as if to promise that there would never be rain again. She stared at the small haze of the candles on the altar, but she did not pray. It was enough to try and straighten out in her mind that she had tried to steal the king's gold and the queen had forgiven her with all her heart. But she could not do it again, forgiveness or not, so now she had no gold and no idea how she might come by any. Moreover, she was freshly bewildered by Queen Margaret's kindness and forgiveness, and by her loving picture of the brutal and ferocious Malcolm as some one who would jest "to tease her."

In a while she gave up trying to understand, and came out of the small dim church to the sunshine. She would just have to be patient and see what each day might bring. Gold might not be so easily come by after all.

o Merca lived in Dunfermline Palace through the long days of the declining summer, drawn in spite of her determined hatred into the happy life that revolved around the queen. There were many times when she had to make a deliberate effort to fight against a treacherous happiness that began to take her unawares. These were days of still, splendid sunshine that hazed the distant blue sea and the hills beyond the Forth, followed by long, limpid twilights when all colors held an aching brilliance, and in the falling dusk, bats swooped around the thatch while the last sleepy birds chittered from the shelter of the glen. Whenever she could, she would take Dag's hand and walk with him to the high grass above the tower, determined to be alone with him as much as possible, but she could no longer separate herself from the small world laid out below her.

The pale walls of the new tower had risen through the summer to be crowned now with its roof. In the carpenter's sheds down at the bottom of the hill where the sweet-smelling timber was stacked to dry, the men were fashioning furniture for the dwelling rooms that would be provided above the stores and the servants' quarters; rooms that would be as pleasing and beautiful as Queen Margaret could make them, even if the tower was, as her husband wished, no more than a stronghold pierced with arrow slits, dark and windowless for easy defence. More slowly, the pale stone rectangle of the church was rising down the hill, for Malcolm did not have his wife's faith that all troubles with his enemies could be smoothed by words, and he insisted that the tower come first. Around and below the two buildings of fresh-cut stone sprawled the wood and wattle huddle of the palace, scattered on the darkening hillside with light springing here and there among the shadows, and the soft twanging of a harp from one of the dwellings falling soft against the clang of a hammer on an anvil, where the smiths worked late in the glow of the distant forge.

These were the treacherous moments for Merca, when the quiet evening cloaked her, and the long day had been content and busy, rich in the pleasure of her growing skills and warmed by the gentle presence of the queen. Dag spoke beside her on one such evening, and brought her sharply from the mood of content into which she had been slipping.

"When I am big here," he said dreamily, looking down over his hunched-up knees at the spread acres of the palace, "I could be a monk like these ones, or be a soldier, or just be a gentleman like Mary's brother Dougal who does not do anything but just be there when the Queen wants him. They would teach me to be anything I want."

He spoke more easily now, finding words to clothe his thoughts; but Merca did not care about his words, as she jerked around on him in sharp horror.

"You will not stay here till you are big!"

Dag looked at her in surprise and suddenly she noticed how he had grown, his round face beginning to lengthen a little under the long, thick thatch of his hair.

"Why?" was all he said, but his sister saw the dangerous darkening of his eyes, and knew better now than to push him until she had some definite plan to offer, and at the moment she had to admit ruefully that she had no plans at all.

"Because," she said lamely, "we cannot take things from someone else all our lives. We must learn to look after ourselves."

Dag's lower lip came out, for he could remember some of that business of looking after themselves, and it did not seem to him very good. But at the moment he did not have to argue, for below the bell began to swing in the rough timber tower and it was time for them to walk down through the cooling dusk and into the little church for the evening prayer with all the household. Dag ran at once, delighted to get away from trouble, and Merca followed him more slowly.

Nor did she surrender herself to the peace of the little church, lined with bowed heads in the soft blaze of the candles. She bent her own head into her hands but she was far from prayer, her mind whirling with self-reproach. All summer she had been here with this king at her hand, and watching his genial and good-natured face about his homestead, she had almost come to forget who he was and all that he had done; begun to forget even that she herself was from ravaged Northumbria. She was even slipping into the Gaelic tongue more easily than her own; forgetting, forgetting, forgetting. Now Dag had brought her to her senses. He was very small, and he had forgotten so much that he looked to this country and these people for all the rest of his life. Through the soft drone of vesper and response she lifted her head and looked all round her; she looked bitterly at the dark red head of Malcolm bent beside the red-gold of his slender queen. She now felt dimly that in addition to everything else, they had stolen Dag, who would be glad to grow up to be a Scot. All her hatred boiled up afresh and she could not think how she had ever forgotten it. If she prayed for anything in the church that evening, with the candles starlike on the altar, and the thrushes fluting in the dusk outside, and the cool, damp scents of summer coming through the open door, it was that she might be a better hater than she had ever been, and that someone might help her with a plan for killing.

Help came much sooner than she had dared to hope, in a form which threw the tranquil Palace of Dunfermline into an anxious turmoil. She herself saw the horseman who brought the first news come thundering up the beaten track through the buildings, heedless of any who might be in his way, with his cloak flying above the flanks of his mud-spattered horse. She was going down to the monastery in the hour approaching noon, and like everybody else she had to leap from his path, turning to watch him as he wheeled unchecked into the courtyard and flung himself from the saddle outside the great door of the hall. Even at that distance, she could hear him shouting for the king. All around the palace, people seemed to have sprung out of the ground as he passed, gathering in small knots with their questioning faces turned towards the hall. But the noon bell was already ringing, and

Merca shrugged and went on her way, for what did she care about the business of this king? She had enough to do with the business of the queen, whose bounty had become so far known that each day the poor and hungry came crowding to her doors six and seven hundred strong, nor were they ever turned away, but given the queen's charity and the queen's blessing, with the gold now provided bountifully by her husband. Merca's daily task with her baskets of bread had grown heavier, but even the memory that she was once like them could never lift her to pity for the draggled, snuffling horde that stood each day beyond the monastery gates. She did as she was bidden, and then she forgot them, as if in her dark, determined hatred, her heart was dead to everyone except Dag.

This day there was an air of suppressed excitement among the ladies who fed the poor, as they looked at each other over their heads in anxiety and surmise, glancing constantly at the door as if they hoped or expected that someone would come.

It was Dougal who came in the end, whirling in to grasp his sister by the arms, his eyes bright with excitement above his curling beard.

"It is war!" he cried. "It is war, sweet sister!" His cheerful face belied his grave words.

"Oh Dougal, how can you look so pleased! Who would want another battle?"

Dougal had the grace to look a little shamefaced, wiping the pleasure from his eyes, and standing more soberly.

"It cannot be avoided, Mary," he said. "When our King fought for the Queen's brother Aedgar, his kinsman

Gospatric turned traitor and went south to make peace with Norman William, and for this treachery the Norman gave him Northumbria. This you know."

Mary nodded, but her face was sad and her eyes heavy.

"Well, our good Master Gospatric walks like a bantam in the Norman favor and has been so bold as to invade the edges of our southern kingdom. This cannot be, sister, and you know it. The king must ride. Besides—" He looked shamefaced again and fingered the edges of his checkered cloak which he held bundled in his arms—"Besides, this woman's court grows a little wearying, and our swords are blunt. We take to the saddle gladly! Now I must be away to the forge to see my man gets a proper edge to my broadsword. I will see you to bid you farewell!"

He swirled out as cheerfully as he had swirled in, and Mary looked after him, her teeth biting on her lower lip.

"But Dougal," she said hopelessly, even though he could not hear her. "The Queen—!"

It was the only day that Merca knew the queen to fail to come and help in the feeding of the poor who were her especial care, and when she saw her in her place at the evening meal her face was deathly white and her eyes red and tender as if she had been weeping. Merca had no care for the queen's grief, filled as she was with a delighted exulting hope that perhaps some Saxon or Norman sword would take her vengeance for her, and she need fret no more about her search for gold and Thomas of the Knife. Glancing at the queen's pale face she felt a sudden unwilling pang of pity; perhaps if the king were out of the way there would be no need to hate the queen, who had not herself done any harm.

She stood with Dag to see them go in the first blue gray light of morning, when the white mist still hung in wreaths and tendrils through the dark trees of the glen and the sun was only a red glow above the shadowed country to the east. All the night long the palace had echoed with the clang of hammers and the clash of arms as weapons were sharpened and burnished and horses were freshly shod against the long journey; and all through the dark hours men's voices had defeated sleep. Now as the pale shape of the tower drew the first light from the morning, and candles were snuffed in the windows of the palace, they were all gone; rising up like a tide over the slope at the top of the glen in a sea of hooves and moving flanks and chiming weapons. The tip of Malcolm's sword was caught by the first sun as he stood in his stirrups at the crest of the rise, and lifted it in farewell to the queen, who stood in sadness and silence beside the rising stones of her new church.

"Perhaps he will get killed."

Merca could not resist voicing her eager hopes to Dag, who looked at her in surprise, and she could not explain to him how the sight of the mass of Scots in their saffron shirts and plaided cloaks, with their steel caps crammed down on their long, wild hair, had brought back to her all the fear and horror of Wearmouth, so that in the dreadful clarity of her memories she hated Malcolm afresh, as if it had all happened yesterday. Dag had no such memories to trouble him. Most of these soldiers were now his friends, and he had enjoyed the morning, deeply excited in some way by the trampling horses and the shouting men, the dull weapons in the early light, and the cold, cheerful faces of the soldiers themselves. As in all moments of feeling, his fingers ran around the edges of his shell, and he stood with feet braced wide apart and eyes shining, his small fat stomach stuck out over his leather belt; in that moment he was himself a soldier.

"Kings do not get killed," he said loftily. "Who would dare to kill a king!"

Merca looked at him and knew, with her young heart as cold as the morning, that she would dare, for his sake. Only this would bring Dag close to her again as they had once been—but how much simpler it would be if someone would do it for her in this battle.

No one, however, succeeded in taking on her task, and Merca stood with the smiling and rejoicing household in a bitter March wind to see them all ride home again. They were laden to the last overburdened pack horse, and staggering under bundles of booty larger than any they had ever dragged home before. In the excited crowd there were only two faces that showed no sign of rejoicing. Merca looked at the jewels and the clothes and the household treasures and even the children's toys that dripped from the baggage of the soldiers, and knew them to come from other households in Northumbria that had been exactly like her own, and her desire for vengeance surged in her as strongly and bitterly as it had when she first came to Dunfermline. And the queen, as she greeted her grin-

ning and victorious Malcolm, was in tears, as conscious as Merca of all the homesteads that had flamed into the sky to make this triumphant return.

Through the following weeks, the girl fretted in her fresh anger and thought how she might gain her gold and reach her purpose, but, once again, the threat was taken out of her hands. Gospatric was now William's henchman, and his rout by Malcolm brought the Norman revenge as sharp and swift as the counterthrusting of a sword. The Conqueror himself came riding northwards with his son Robert, at the head of the vast Norman cavalry, lances glittering like ice in the sun and their hooves like thunder up through conquered England. At the same time from the sea, the square-sailed painted Norman warships drove into the estuary of the River Tay, and Malcolm and his Palace of Dunfermline lay between the jaws of the fiercest Norman trap yet laid for Scotia.

"My love, we must go from here." Fresh from his attempts to stem the Norman army, Malçolm came to Margaret with his difficult decision. "Whichever way I turn to fight, then the other arm of their attack can take me in the rear, and I dare not divide my army. The position is untenable. We must leave Dunfermline, and I will take you and all the women and children to shelter in the monastery of Dunkeld until the threat is over. We will ourselves defend Scotia from the hills of Atholl, and it will take more than Norman William to shake us out of there."

Margaret was silent, looking at him across the shadows of her bower, where the candles were not yet lit in a chilly dusk, and the smoke from the fire blew and eddied in cold circles around the comfortless room. Yet it was all the home that she had ever known with Malcolm, and more precious to her than the finest palace of stone; she found it difficult in this moment to be a queen, facing him with her head up to take whatever might come, without complaint.

"My poor?" was all she said, a little faintly. "What of them?"

Malcolm tried not to look impatient, conscious of the Norman hordes advancing steadily towards Fife.

"The monks will care for them. Nor will they leave, for they are in no danger. The Normans respect them."

Malcolm marched up and down like a penned bull, his head down and his anxious feet kicking up the rushes behind him, and she smiled to see how desperately he needed her to make it easy for him. Never before had he had to meet threat of war in fear and anguish for those he loved and the household he would have to leave behind him. Until now, fear had been a matter for other people —not for himself—and Malcolm's haggard and troubled face was more than the queen could bear. Cheerfully she stood up, huddling her cloak around her against the drafts.

"Well, my husband," she said, "if we are to go, we had better get prepared." Then she smiled at the childish relief on his face, as he picked up her hands and kissed them.

"I am unused," he said, "to considering women in my wars. I had no idea what you might say. Now we must make all possible speed."

Despite all the queen's efforts at serenity, it was a strangely silent cavalcade that struggled out over the hill two days later into the cold lash of wind-driven rain. There was none of the excitement with which the men had ridden against Gospatric, and the whole procession straggled along at the different paces of horses and pack animals, baggage wagons and litters; servants and dependants with their families and all their worldly possessions heaped upon their backs; herds of confused cattle and great rumbling wagons sticking in the mud, laden with all the household goods of the royal court of Scotia.

Merca waited tranquilly and with a high heart through the days they spent packed into the guest house of the great monastery in Dunkeld, indifferent to all discomfort in her certainty that against the Normans, Malcolm stood in real danger of his death. She did not care who defeated the Scots as long as they were beaten into the earth.

Dag, as always, had no thoughts of vengeance. For a while his fingers were nervous around his shell as he listened to the anxious chatter of the ladies, but he soon found contentment when he wandered into the monastery itself and found there monks exactly the same as those he had grown to love in Dunfermline.

"With circles on their heads, too," he said to Merca happily. Merca looked at him in bafflement and was for a moment tempted to pour out all her plans of vengeance and death for the King of Scotia, but some new strength she sensed in Dag held her back; some fear that he might come out firmly against her and then she would be more alone than ever.

She would have waited less hopefully in the packed and noisy guest house if she had been able to see through the rain-driven hills to the scene of what should have been Malcolm's battle with the invading Normans.

From the close-growing woods on the north bank of the Tay, he and his men peered desperately out at the painted ships rocking gently in the wide river mouth, and at the glowing campfires that drew ever nearer over on the hills of Fife, announcing the coming of the Norman army. In the end, it came no closer than the south banks of the river, and the rain stopped so that the long-massed ranks of spear and breastplate and cone-shaped cap glittered more brightly than the water in the spring sunshine. But one boat alone crossed the wide, smooth river, with only a handful of knights and one tall figure who towered above all the rest. This man splashed ashore when the boat grounded under the eyes of the astonished Scots. His hands were empty at his sides and his sword and spear were left behind him in the boat.

"You are being trapped!" the older men cried to Malcolm, and would have held him back. "Do not go, my lord, it is a trap!" But Malcolm shook them from his arms.

"You shame me," he cried. "The man bears no arms! Besides," he added, peering out of the thicket through the first flush of young green. "Besides—I like his looks."

Merca's fairest hopes came to an end when Malcolm walked out from his sheltering woods, unarmed himself, to meet the son of Norman William, and he and Robert faced each other on the pebbly shore, each as tall as the other; each a man of character and candor; each liking what he saw in the other's face. At the small nearby town of Abernethy they signed a peace for Scotia and Norman England, and for the first time the queen's prayers were answered, and the differences between the two kingdoms were settled only with words. The straight-backed, somber Normans in their steel nose pieces and their long bright tunics stared at the kilted saffron-shirted Scots, and they stared back above their flowing whiskers at the dark clean-shaven faces of their new friends. Between Malcolm and Robert a bond was made that needed no signing: the immediate friendship of two honest men who had measured each other and found the answer good.

It was Dag who told Merca about it all and she did not believe him.

"No battle!" she cried, appalled. "What do you mean, no battle?"

"It is as I said," Dag repeated. "The whole place rejoices because there has been no battle."

"What do you mean?" she cried again. "How can two armies meet and there be no battle? What of the King?"

"The King is here. I have seen him." He looked at his sister, unable to understand her baffled and angry face. As long as his own small world went well, he did not concern himself much with the larger one, but surely it was a good thing if there had been no battle. People did not get killed and there were no women weeping. Dimly he remembered a time when he knew much more of things like this, but he did not like to think of it.

"How do you know there was no battle?" Her fists were

142

clenched with frustration. So much promise, and somehow it had slipped her grasp.

"I was helping Brother Ambrose clean the fishpond." He looked down at the green stains on his tunic which would somehow have to be explained to Mary later. "We had a net and—"

"Never mind about the fishpond! Tell me of the battle —or not battle."

Dag looked affronted. No battle could measure against the bliss of his rolled-up sleeves and the cold stone of the parapet underneath his stomach while his arm groped in the green slippery water for the green slippery fish. And Brother Ambrose beside him saying small Latin prayers and then darting at the fish with his net, and then praying again and darting again and getting quite angry with God because he could not catch the fish and his habit was getting wet. He sighed. Merca was never interested in the really exciting things.

"A man came from the kitchen," he said as shortly as possible. "He said to Brother Ambrose that the King had made friends with the Normans and we could all go home. Brother Ambrose said thank God for that," he added.

"Made friends with the *Normans*," Merca echoed, as though he had said, "Made friends with the devil." "And we can all go *where?*" she added, furiously.

"Home," Dag said innocently. "Home to Dunfermline. Where else? I am in a hurry to go, for Father Gregory has promised me that soon I shall paint in color. Red, I think, or blue."

He stood there unthinking on the stone steps of the formal garden, his eyes vague on the brown slopes of the mountains, lost in the happy decision between blue and green and red, and Merca stood below him and looked at him with tears rising to her eyes.

Home to Dunfermline! Home, indeed!

She knew bitter triumph when they came to the end of their happy journey back to Dunfermline. She was one of the first to cross the ridge of hill that looked down on the palace, riding behind one of the gentlemen-in-waiting to the king. As they crested the ridge and drew rein, neither Malcolm nor Margaret uttered a single word, staring in silence down at their homestead while around them women shrieked and men shouted and cursed with their hands flying to the hilt of their swords, and somewhere Merca could hear the loud angry voice of the queen's mother already lifted in abuse and lamentation.

Down below them, the Palace of Dunfermline was no more than drifting heaps of blackened ash with nothing but the scarred outlines to show where the buildings had been standing. Only the monastery farther down the hill was unscathed. The clean stone of the new tower was blackened with the blown smoke and even the windlasses of the new building were collapsed in charred sticks over foundations filled with drifted ash. There had been peace with the Normans on their way home, but they had left their mark behind them on their march north.

Fierce, desperate exultation filled Merca, and a blinding recollection of the smoke rising from her own home, and of the charred houses and the pitiful piles of ash in Wearmouth, with Malcolm and his men striding through them without a sideways glance. Now he would know, she thought, with a rush of pleasure that was like a giddiness. Now he will know! At last it had happened to him. The Normans had not taken his life as she had hoped, but they had taken his home, which was the next best thing, and she peered eagerly around the back of the man in front of her so that she could see his face as he gave way to grief and rage. The wails of the Princess Agatha rose above the weeping of all the other women, and the men grumbled and cursed and threatened, but the king and queen sat quite still, and in her litter the queen shifted the sleeping baby Edward on her arm as if she had nothing else to think of. It was she who spoke first and her smile was as sweet and strong as if it cost her no effort.

"I never liked it, Malcolm my heart," she said. "You know that. And now you can have the satisfaction of telling me how right you were to build the tower before the church. We can live in that while we build ourselves a new stone palace worthy of the King of Scotia, instead of a clutter of wattle huts where an army camped. We will have the noblest dwelling in all our land and furnish it to match, and dress ourselves in cloth of gold."

The eyes she turned on him were more brilliant than her smile, glittering with the tears she would not shed.

"With jewels on, sweet Margaret," Malcolm said. "With jewels on," and it sounded as if he had difficulty in finding his voice.

Merca turned and hid her face, cheated and disappointed and filled with the same desolation that had struck her when Dag spoke of these ruins as his home.

t was as though the household in Dunfermline in those days of early summer
was determined to resist all Merca's hopes
that they should be overborne with sorrow. First, with the
new leaves bursting on the trees above the ruins and the
young grass leaping to overgrow the scars of sadness, the
palace rejoiced in the birth of the queen's second son. Ed-
mund, they called him, after the great warrior who had
been Queen Margaret's grandfather, and Mary brought
Merca and Dag to see him where he lay in the nursery in
the great carved cradle of Malcolm's Viking ancestors.
Dag smiled and laid a finger on the small red puckered
cheek exactly as he touched in passing the kittens that
rolled in the sun around the granary door, but Merca
glared at the baby and knew only the memory of Dag.
She remembered the infant Dag quite clearly, but she
could no longer remember by any effort the clear face of
the mother who had bent above him. It was as if something else had been stolen from Merca, and Mary looked
in despair at her frozen face, amazed that even the sleeping baby could not touch her. As Dag had made it clear
that this place was his home, Merca was locked in a lonely
hate more bitter than any she had known, nor was there
any danger of her drifting through the days toward forget-
fulness as she had drifted in the previous summer. It was
like a darkness that walked with her through all the
brightness of the days, and closed her off from everyone
around her.

All the soft blue days of the young season were busied with the furnishing of the dwelling rooms in the tower, for the queen was true to her word and would not live in them in their barren state. She summoned all the foreign merchants who plied in and out of the wide waters of the Forth, and planned to offer them the goods of Scotland in exchange for their silks and tapestries and fine furnishings. There was to be gold and silver on the tables for their meals and fine carved chairs for them to sit in, padded in velvets and soft skins, and candles of fine white wax to light them in the evenings, banishing forever the reek of tallow that had fought with the turf smoke in Malcolm's wattle home. Charmed, her ladies flocked about her and talked and twittered over the merchants' wares, and the days of sewing were longer and busier than ever. Malcolm stepped cautiously among it all with his big feet and raised his rough red eyebrows at the coming splendor.

"And why not, my lord?" The queen looked up at him, smothered in yards of crimson velvet, new from France, that she struggled to straighten in its folds. Her veil was a little awry and her face flushed with her efforts. Malcolm smiled and took the other end of the material in his big hands to help her, and the ladies giggled to see him. "And why not?" she went on earnestly. "Is there some particular good in being ugly? If that were the case then our old court must have been filled with virtue!" She went on shrewdly, "And mark you, Malcolm, it will do much for our trade, for soon the people will copy us and splendor will be the fashion, and we can send abroad in exchange the things we have plenty of, like our furs and our fine woolen cloth."

Her lovely face glowed, and Malcolm smiled and let her have her way, even submitting with fair grace to all his own new clothes that she insisted on.

"It is time," she said, "that we had you looking like a king, and less like some rough soldier new come from the glens."

He glanced a little longingly at his discarded tunic, the leather patched to hide the wear and sword cuts of many years.

"I am but a rough soldier," he said. "Dear Margaret, do not think too highly of me."

"You are a king."

Their happiness colored the whole atmosphere of the court, and the soft air of the young summer was filled with plans and projects and gay light-heartedness, and through it all Merca walked as if she were sealed inside her own shadow where the sun of happiness could not touch her. Even Dag, growing older and shrewder, noticed it, and treated her warily. He was deeply happy in this place and saw nothing that he could not love in the genial and good-humored king and the gentle soft-spoken queen, and the quiet monks who taught him such wonderful things, and Mary, whose merry kindness was like a warm cushion to fall back on when anything went wrong. He was frightened of his sister's cold hatred of these people who were good to him; frightened that somehow she could take it all away. So he avoided her as much as possible and talked nervously when they were together of things that did not matter. Merca watched him and the cold pain inside her grew even sharper, for she knew now that she had lost Dag, and when they told her in the high days of summer that she was going to leave him for a while, she hardly even protested; it was foolish any more to say that Dag could not live alone when he was already gone from her. Almost in a trance of indifference she listened to the plans with which the court was humming.

"It is high time, my Margaret," Malcolm said, plowing his way through the piles of silks and samples of carving and silver plates that heaped the new rooms of the tower. "It is high time you left all this a while and came with me to visit my western kingdom, and let my people see their Queen."

The queen put down her embroidery frame and looked at him across a sea of bright cushions.

"Oh, Malcolm," was all she said, but her blue eyes glowed with excitement.

"The babes are well," the king went on, "and can safely be left with your mother. All this,"—he waved a hand about the cluttered chamber and leaped to grab a candlestick as he swept it off a table. "All this will get done without you now. I thought we would go as far west as the lands the Northmen have but this year returned to me—for you, my love, who love all holy places, there is there the holiest place in all our kingdom. It is an island called Iona."

Now the queen's eyes were wide and steady. "Tell me of it."

Malcolm eased a heap of velvet and a pile of ermine

trimmings off a stool and kicked a spool of gold thread half across the floor, and as he sat down beside her even his rough, practical face grew a little distant.

"I know but little. It is the island of Columcille, who brought word of God to Scotia, the holy place where he first set his feet and built his monastery. There the Kings of Scotia are buried, and I understand their bones lie undisturbed, for all the ravages of the Northmen."

"Columcille," said Margaret softly, as though the name itself was music. "I have heard of him a little, a warrior first and then a saint. He laid aside his sword for God."

Malcolm looked at her sharply, as if he thought her last remark for him, but her eyes were wide and absent, piercing the bare stone walls to something far beyond.

"I am told," Malcolm went on, "that he was so huge a man that no follower of his came ever past his shoulder, and his voice for all its beauty so tremendous that it could be heard across the water of the Sound of Mull, and that a full mile wide."

Margaret turned now and smiled at him broadly and her teasing eyes were wide. "Why, Malcolm," she said, "has a saint moved you to admiration? He must indeed have been a man! But I must not hope for too much, since he was also a warrior."

Malcolm grinned and looked down at his feet.

"We will go then to Iona?" he said, lifting his red head.

"We will go to Iona."

There was bustle and commotion through the overcrowded tower as the company was chosen for the long expedition and the new clothes finished and the baggage packed. To her intense amazement, Merca was told she was to go with the party waiting on the queen.

"I?" she asked Mary in astonishment when she was told. "Why should I go on this journey?"

"The Queen thought you would enjoy it," Mary said as brightly as she could, looking with pity at the girl's face, almost as thin now with this nameless unhappiness as it had been with starvation when she came. It was useless to explain that the queen, thoughtful as always for her foster children, had decided it might be a good thing for her to leave Dag for a while, and get away from his obvious happiness in a place that seemed to bring her nothing but some discontent.

"We will take her, Mary," the queen said, never too busy to think of the well-being of even the least of her subjects. "She is nearly fourteen now, and old enough to be sensible and useful on such a journey, and it may be that the new places and the fresh winds of the west will blow away her sadness."

Dag did not mind her going. Like the queen, although he could not put it into words, he thought it might be good to have Merca away for a little while, for she dragged at his contentment with her mournful face.

"You will be happy, sweet sister," he said, and kissed her a little guiltily, and Merca wanted to abuse him for his treachery, but somehow now she did not even seem to have the energy to get cross with Dag. She could not pretend, however, not to be pleased with her new gowns for the journey, one rich deep red and one as green as summer grass, bordered with soft bands of fur that Dag

stroked with loving fingers. They were a new strange shape, close fitting down to her waist with a great bell of a skirt that fell almost to the ground, swirling when she moved, and a new white veil of some material so fine that when she drew it across her face she could see everything still as clearly as if it was not there. The queen had new gowns too and so did Mary, all in the same shape, and Mary told the astonished Merca that they were made after the Norman fashion, for the queen was very up-to-date and wanted no more of these Saxon shapeless shifts, tied around the waist with a girdle like a piece of rope about a sack.

It was a bright and happy company that gathered on the grassy slope below the tower on a day when no rain fell but the dead sky was full of it. Despite the queen's efforts to make her husband's way of life more kingly, the departure from his palace was still cheerful and informal with no man taking place before the other, no matter who he might be. When Merca looked down from where she clung to the back of Dougal, excited and a little tearful at this last moment, Dag was standing beside the king, who struggled, unaided, with the stiff gold buckles of his new sword belt.

"Good-bye, little brother," she cried, and suddenly, she did not want to leave him. Dag looked up, squinting against the gray light of the sky. There was a smear of scarlet down the front of his tunic and a patch of yellow in his hair.

"God speed you, sister," he cried in return, but his mind was not on her going. "See," he added, "the Fathers have let me at the colors and I have painted my shell!"

He held it up for her to see, but because she was too high and distant on Dougal's restless horse, he turned to the person nearest to him. Anyone would do to praise his lovely colors.

"See," he cried again, "I have painted my shell. Oh, it is still wet!"

He laughed, as he seldom did, and lifted his amused face and his outspread red and yellow fingers to the man beside him. Malcolm grunted with satisfaction as he pushed the last buckle into place and looked down at the laughing child. He would have laughed with the devil himself today, and, like most manly men, a friendly word to children came easy to him. Looking down at the round, fair face, his great deep laugh boomed out over the infectious treble as he pulled the boy to him for a moment, and his big hand ruffled his hair.

"Well," he said, "keep your colored fingers to yourself, and off my new cloak, or Madam the Queen will have your bones and mine!"

Merca stared at them in appalled surprise, at Dag laughing up with fearless confidence into the face of their enemy, happiness and content a bond between them for one short, perfect moment. Speechless, she laid her head against Dougal's back and closed her eyes against a tide of misery that seemed to shake her very bones. She did not look at Dag again, and in a few minutes he shrugged and wandered off into the crowd, still smiling as he looked at his red and yellow fingers.

In a few moments more the queen came out from the

tower, radiant in her new gown and cloak and with the softness of the new-fashioned fragile veil drifting about her face. Quietness fell on the crowd as the king helped her into the high, comfortable wooden saddle of her gentle horse, and at the last moment when she was settled, she lifted her eyes to one of the narrow windows of the tower, where the Princess Agatha stood with a baby on each arm. Beside her proud husband, she rode out then at the head of the long, gay cavalcade, to begin the royal progress to the west.

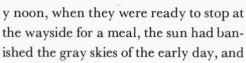

y noon, when they were ready to stop at the wayside for a meal, the sun had banished the gray skies of the early day, and they halted in a blue haze of midday heat along the side of a forest ride where the pigeons cooed in the shadows and the air was heavy with the scent of pines. The ride ran straight and clear away in both directions between the spiked ranks of the trees, and there seemed small possibility of danger, but Malcolm nevertheless ordered his captains to dispose the men at arms so that there was a party on either side of them, watching each approach.

"Though I cannot think," he said, looking at the warm flush of the sun on his wife's face, "that anyone could find an enemy in you."

Margaret smiled down at him. "All the same, I thank my lord for his care," she said, and held out a hand for him to lift her to the ground.

Behind them came the troop of thegns and noblemen like Dougal, whom the queen had persuaded Malcolm to have always in attendance as was fitting to his rank, and among them Merca waited behind Dougal, anxious for him to let her down, for she felt stiff and a little weary after the long morning's ride. They had to draw aside a moment to let pass the company of men-at-arms who were to guard them on the other side, and idly Merca watched them come. Suddenly she froze into attention as she caught sight of a face in the last rank to pass them by. Dougal spoke but she did not hear him.

"Child," he cried then, twisting in the saddle to see what was wrong with her. "I said grasp my waist and let yourself down. What goes wrong?"

Merca stared up at him vacantly and for a long time did not understand what he was saying.

"Forgive me, Dougal," she said at last, and did as he had bidden her, sliding forward carefully so that she might not startle the horse by landing beside his hind legs. She moved as if automatically, not knowing what she did, with a strange blind look on her face, and when her feet were on the short heathery turf she stood quite still, blind to the warm sunshine and with all the light vanished from the sky. Darkness was around her and in the firelight a deep whispering voice was saying "To kill a king. I want to kill a king." How long she had been fretting and scheming and hoping to find gold enough to let Thomas of the Knife fulfill his dream, hope growing a little less with every day even though hate grew no less. And here was Thomas, riding in the cavalcade, and what was he here for if not to kill the king?

Excitement rose in her then like yeast in the dough along the warm shelves of the palace bakery, so that she found it difficult to keep still and not to shout at the king with fierce delight that, at length, his time was come. She gripped her hands together to calm herself, but when she sat down beside Mary in the dappled shadows of the trees, her face was brightly flushed and she felt sick, turning from the good food that the girl unfolded from its napkins.

Mary was concerned that she was not well, bothered by

the thought of sickness at this early stage of the journey and feeling her forehead constantly for a fever. Impatiently Merca shook off her hand. She was sick with this boiling, triumphant excitement, but she felt her spirits rising to dispel all the heavy dullness of these last months in Dunfermline. Surely if Thomas had contrived to get himself among the men at arms then she only had to wait. There was no one else he could be after. Vengeance would be hers only for the waiting; vengeance for her dead mother and father, her smoking home, all the hunger and misery that followed, and Dag grown old and wretched, and not able to remember Christmas. Her mind leapt aside here for she knew there was something that did not fit, but she pushed away the picture of the plump and laughing Dag that she had just left, and clung to the memory of the starving child on the farm.

She could not keep still, and begged Mary to let her walk up and down a while to stretch her legs. She must make quite sure that it was Thomas.

"Very well." Mary was doubtful. "But do not disturb the King and Queen, and do not, whatever you do, go from my sight."

She had no need to go from Mary's sight. The soldiers were not far away and she was known to many of them; nothing was more natural than to go to them and stop to speak. She watched some of them munch their hunks of bread and meat as they stood among their horses with their weapons stacked and their heads bare to the sun, and others on guard along the ride and in among the trees. Thomas lounged against the bare stripped branches

158

of a fallen tree, his steel cap hooked on a stump beside him and a piece of bread and cheese in his hands, eating idly with his crumpled face indifferent to everything that went on around him. Merca looked down at her crimson gown with its bands of fur and laid a hand on her fine veil, and knew that she need have no anxiety that he would know her for the starveling scarecrow of the forest night. She thought he did not make a very convincing soldier, but then of course, only she knew that he was not one, and there was no mistake that it was Thomas. It was impossible not to know the creased, fleshy face and the dark unruly hair. It was impossible to contain her hard satisfied pleasure, and she skipped back to Mary, who looked at her doubtfully and then smiled, putting it all down to the excitement of the journey.

All through the long days of the royal progress she watched and waited. It was as if she was alone in this gay, richly dressed throng with two people; the king, riding content and indifferent at the head of his train, and Thomas of the Knife riding at the back of it among the soldiers. She alone waited for the moment when these two would come together.

To kill a king! To kill a king!

The words echoed to the thump of hoofbeats through the days and filled the darkness around her in the nights, and she watched every movement of the escorting soldiers with ceaseless vigilance so that she might be aware of the moment when it came. So remorselessly did she watch and wait that she saw nothing else. Before they turned westwards, Malcolm took his queen across the Forth to the great escarpment fortress of Dunedin, and Merca alone, because she did not see, remained untouched by the sight of the queen's slow progress up the long slopes to the landward side of the fort, her horse surrounded and overwhelmed by the clamoring masses of the Saxons who had fled into this area in their thousands after the Norman conquest. They followed Queen Margaret in pushing disorder, thrusting forward their children for her to bless and their poor for her to pity, and even their sick for her to heal, for such was the fame now of her gentle holiness that belief was growing in the healing of her touch.

In the middle of the press, wearied by her pity for their sufferings, and oppressed with humility and despair that they should think this of her, she turned to Malcolm.

"For who am I?" she asked him in distress, "that they should think this of me? Why should they feel my touch is holy?"

"Ah, why indeed?" Malcolm answered as he struggled to protect her from the clamoring crowd who pressed around her, struggling against each other even to touch the furred hem of her gown. "Why indeed, my sweet one, except that word has gone round the kingdom that you love them, every single one of them, as much sometimes as I think you love me."

He struggled with a light answer to ease the burden they laid on her by her love of all human creatures, but it lay too heavy for her and, in the end, looking at her pale, distraught face he was forced to have his men disperse the people that he might carry her away and gain her some peace.

At the front of the company the queen suffered from the burden of those who made their claims on her; in the middle of the company among the gentlemen-in-waiting, Merca's heart was closed even to the thought of love by her festering hate; and at the back, among the men at arms, Thomas of the Knife neither loved nor hated, but planned his work, the gold of his down payment from a petty enemy jingling in his pouch, and his mind fixed on his long ambition to kill a king.

As they rode toward the west, there was relief from the pursuing crowds, the settlements grew few and far between in this wilder part of Scotia so that there were only scattered villagers to come running in groups from their reed-thatched huts to stare with wide astonished eyes at the brilliant cavalcade; and to run for miles beside their smiling queen along the stony tracks of their bleak country. The company spent the nights in the barren forts and watchtowers of Malcolm's thegns, with Margaret's clucking ladies snatching what comfort they could for her in the bare uncompromising chambers with their cold, sweating walls and beds of damp piled heather. Through every day or night, Merca waited even when she could see neither Thomas nor the king, listening with eagerness for the uproar and the shouting and the consternation that would follow the killing of a king.

By the time that they took ship from the small, huddled port of Glasgu, she had come to the conclusion that Thomas meant to wait until they were in the far isolation of the island before he lifted his knife, and she hugged herself to think of his cleverness. There had been a lot of talk of this Iona, and she had gathered that it was little more than a rock abandoned in the western seas, something to do with some saint or other and with hardly anybody living on it. What an excellent place for Thomas to do his work, far from any help for a dying king, far from Dunfermline and indeed from Malcolm's kingdom itself so that time must pass before even the news of it could reach Scotia. She knew a few moments of sick alarm when she realized that there was only one ship sailing for Iona and that the number of men at arms to be carried would be very few; but relief came when she saw Thomas walking up the narrow gangplank, one of the chosen few.

In the beauty of the journey she was almost able to forget vengeance and death; and the queen sat entranced through every waking hour on her carved chair in the bows of the boat that skidded with its white sails flying down the wide blue waters of the Clyde. On one hand the steep hills crowded purple to the sea's edge with a few scattered villages clinging to the shore below them and the heather on their rounded crests stained pink and gold and orange by the sun that shone across them on to the fair open farm lands, sloping away from the far shore of the river. They crept in the paling sunlight of the afternoon through a narrow, slate-blue channel between the folded hills, where sudden black storm clouds chased their shadows over the sunlit flanks and the rain came, instant and violent, slashing down through the strange purple light to send the delighted queen and her shrieking ladies into shelter. As swiftly as they had come, the clouds raced out above the open sea, leaving the last rain falling through the sunlight in rods of silver and a vast rainbow spanning the hilltops.

"Oh, Malcolm," breathed the Queen, back at once to her place in the prow. "Oh, Malcolm, it is an omen! Such beauty can only be an omen of happiness! I am longing for Iona."

Merca watched from a distance and saw her lovely face flushed with rose from the sun and wind, and her tawny hair tattered into rough curls round the edges of her veil, her gentle blue eyes glowing with happiness at so much of the beauty she loved. For one sudden instant the girl's heart lurched and stopped with sudden understanding of what was going to happen, and in that moment she saw the reality, and knew the grief and anguish that lay ahead. Then the strange veil closed again over her mind, narrowing it to everything except her desire for vengeance, as black and unpitying and deadly as a nightmare.

They moored and spent the night in the shelter of the narrow water, sailing out next morning with the breaking day onto a clear, glittering sea as fresh and brilliant as the dawning of the world. The captain of the ship came up to the king and queen and bade them look to the southwest between the bleached rocky islands that fell to the edges of the sea on small secret beaches that only the sea birds knew. Far beyond the sea that darkened now to the blue depth of the autumn day, they saw the faint purple shadow of the coast of Erin, laid like a stripe of velvet on the surface of the water. Malcolm put an arm around his queen and she pushed back her blowing veil, so that she could see better.

"I asked Father Turgot," she said, and her wide eyes were sad as she looked at the far blue line, "to tell me of Columcille. The greatest warrior in Ireland, he was, the son of kings, but when he was a priest, he forgot his priest-hood and raised the sword. For his penance, he came so far from Erin that he could no longer see even the faint-est smudge of land. I think him wise," she said, "for Malcolm, my love, would it not be heartbreak if that were all that one could see of a beloved country. Better to see nothing."

Erin faded into the blue, shining sea and the ship drove steadily northward on the long steady rising swell of the great ocean that stretched away now to the west of them. The air was so clear and brilliant that it seemed possible to see to the limits of the world, and the translucent water was striped with blue and green and purple, the white seabirds that screamed around the masthead trailing their shadows across it like the brush of feathers.

There were islands here and there, barren folds of rock and stone as old as time itself, but they lay on the moving sea as lightly as the seabirds floating round them, and as if they might just as easily rise and leave it. In the late afternoon the captain came again, and pointed out to them an island no bigger than the rest, lying ahead across a channel from a larger mass of land on which the west-ering sun struck monstrous jagged cliffs and turned them into harmless bastions of fairy rose.

"There it lies, Madam! Across the Sound from the cliffs of Mull."

Queen Margaret did not answer, but stood up to stare

across the sea, and her hands lifted as if, against her will, she reached out to grasp the distant wraith of an island and take it to herself. The wind had dropped by the time they reached it in the early evening, and the water lay across the Sound as clear as glass, barely swelling to the whisper of the rising tide. The astonished company were able to hang over the ship's sides and gaze in wonder at the sea bed, trailed with the dark waving shadows of tangy sea wrack, some two fathoms and a half below her keel. The queen glanced at this for only a moment, smiling at her delighted ladies, and then left them and stood in silence to stare at the small green island opposite them. It sloped with grasslands to the sea, but at each end an outcrop of rock fell on the far side in great cliffs to the open ocean. Here and there were a few small huts, their thatch weighted with heavy stones against the winter gales, and the small hardy sheep of their owners ranged up and down the rugged hills, while a few cows grazed in the gentler fields closer to the sea. The queen's eyes were on the ruins that stood on the grassy slopes above the bone-white beach, their tumbled stones and burned-out timber long smoothed from tragedy by the trees grown through them and the healing carpet of ivy, and the spikes of summer flowers still blooming here in the tardy northern sun. Merca was not far away from her, and looking at her, she could not understand why it was that the queen's eyes were touched with tears at the sight of this place that she had longed for with so much joy.

Malcolm understood why.

"It is the destruction, my heart," she said to him as

later they stood together in the shadows of the ruins, with the seabirds screaming coldly around their heads, and the evening wind blowing from the darkening cliffs of Mull. "I cannot bear to see the destruction, the havoc of violence and the sword in this of all places, the holiest place in all our kingdom." She pushed aside the tall fronds of yellow goldenrod and the thickets of willow herb as pink as the afternoon cliffs beyond the Sound and the clinging trails of ancient roses. Malcolm moved to help her, until they stood looking down on the row of flat stones let into the ground, moss-grown and neglected, the abandoned shrines of the kings of her husband's Scotia, ignored by the invading Vikings when they had tumbled the stones and fired the timbers of the small monastery behind her.

"I suppose," she said sadly, "it is something that they have not been disturbed."

In a moment, she knelt down in the damp grass. Malcolm stood beside her and laid a hand on her shoulder, her soft veil blowing across him, and his hard soldier's face was, for once, as striken by the violence of the wars he loved as was her own. So Merca came upon them unawares, together in the strange unearthly silence of this island that knew no sound but the crying of the seabirds and the faint swelling of the autumn sea, and the memory implanted in its very stones of the voice of Columcille, lifted here to praise God until it echoed in the same evening silence on the far cliffs of Mull.

Once again, Merca was filled suddenly with a great fear that she did not understand, overawed and frightened by the loneliness of the island and the strange silent peace of the kneeling queen with the last sun caught in her red-gold hair, and the king standing so quietly beside her. She knew in an instant of certainty, that there were many things she did not understand, and that the great world of people was not as simple as she had thought it, not all good and not all bad, even for people like Malcolm, but somewhere in between. She turned suddenly and ran, back to the safety of a more normal world where the servants kindled fires against the evening chill and set up camp, where the king and queen would lodge in Iona for as long as the weather remained fair.

"Why Merca, daughter, you are shivering. Here, wrap yourself in this and come closer to the fire." Mary snugged a plaid around her shoulders and led her to a fire that already danced in the fast falling northern dusk with all the blue brilliance of salt-soaked drift. Anxiously she looked at the girl, shaking her head in concern, for she had not seemed well since they set out, and it was small use curing her spirit if they should bring her down with a fever. Merca herself felt hazed with a curious weariness, and for the first time since they had left Dunfermline she gave no thought to where Thomas of the Knife might be in relation to the king.

"It is the air," Mary said when she found Merca drowsing by the fire a little later. "It is so strong up here and tainted with the wrack. Here take your broth now and then sleep, my Merca, and you will be ready for the morning sun."

Merca was too weary even to answer her, wrapped in this overwhelming drowsiness, but obediently she supped the warm broth and after that she made no further effort to stay awake, gratefully allowing Mary to steer her to the bed of piled heather in the cloth pavilion where the ladies were to rest.

She did not know afterward what sound had roused her, but her waking later that night was immediate and urgent, all her heaviness and drowsiness fled, banished by some terror. Her first thought was for Dag, and then she remembered that Dag was not with her, so he could be in no danger here. Around her, the queen's ladies slept on undisturbed, and after a few moments trying to clear her frightened mind, Merca felt driven to get up, some instinct telling her to pick her way in silence between the heather couches and the sleepers on the floor, until she stood outside the pavilion in the star-filled night.

The sky was spilling with stars and their white light seemed to hang immediately above the shadows of the mountains of Mull, and almost to fall into the dark gleaming sea that sighed and murmured on the beach below her. Still she did not know what had awakened her, nor why she had this sense of fear. The night was silent save for the distant footsteps of a sentry, the seagulls quiet, and all the starlight still.

Then a shadow moved, suddenly, between the ladies' pavilion and the vast striped one of the king and queen. Curiously and not yet understanding, Merca moved after it, seeing it in the white muted light to be a man, who crept in stealthy silence toward the doorway of the king. She felt that this was happening in a dream, and although she could not reason who the man might be or what he was about, she knew it was imperative that she must follow him and find out. She crept behind him until he lifted the tent flap of the striped pavilion and vanished inside and a moment later she lifted it herself.

A white flood of starlight fell clear and cold, on the uplifted knife and the dark crumpled face of Thomas. This was the moment of her triumph, but Merca knew only sick horror and shock. Although she had not allowed herself to know it, immersing herself in the darkness of her unreasoning hate, moments of clearness and knowledge had been awakening her mind. Gradually she had come to an unacknowledged understanding that had struck her strongly in that moment beside the graves of the kings; an understanding of the goodness of Malcolm, who was so loved by his gentle wife; an understanding that if he had appeared to do evil things there may have been a reason for them. She was almost walking in her sleep, aroused by this instinct of danger, and her half-conscious mind knew only truth. She did not see her smoking home, or the dreadful monster of her feverishly nourished hate. She saw only the genial red-whiskered face that had laughed down at her little brother, and the quiet man who had stood that evening beside the queen. Her scream of terror pierced Malcolm's sleep before the falling knife could pierce his breast. The king's long soldier's training had taught him to move in sleep almost as quickly as he could move awake, and when Merca screamed, he instantly flung himself sideways, taking Thomas with him to the floor. Blood spread dark across his shirt from a small gash above his ribs, and his shouts alerted the guards until the whole camp was alive with kindled torches and running feet and shouting people. The king was not dead as Merca had so often pictured it, but very much alive, wiping the dead assassin's blood from his own hands and looking down on the appalled child with astonished gratitude, unable to understand from her incoherent words what had come about, but knowing clearly that she had saved his life.

"Let her rest, Malcolm," the queen said. "She will tell us at some time. She is frightened now and shaken."

Later she tried to tell the queen what had happened, but could find no words to describe the strange, lonely darkness in which she had walked through all these long, unhappy months. She only knew that now the darkness had vanished and that the queen's face beside her shone as brightly as in the light of a hundred candles, and that the sun outside also shone as if on a new world. She felt light and tired as when an intolerable burden has lifted.

"I could not sleep," was all she said, and the gentle Queen Margaret smiled at her and wondered why the look of strain and misery was gone from the young face and the girl looked as tranquil and happy as the odd little brother. She shook her head and gave up trying to understand.

"Well, daughter, whatever else befell," she said, "you have the King's gratitude, and also you have my blessing, for he is most precious to me, even as he is precious to all Scotia."

Again she could not understand the wide, weary smile that illuminated the girl's face.

"The Queen's blessing," Merca whispered to herself and sighed with happiness. Now it covered her as it covered everyone else, and she need no longer stand outside. Already she could not think why she had ever done so.

As the queen went out, she thought suddenly of Dag, and now she knew that when she got back to Dunfermline, she and Dag would be once more one.

Dag knew it too, as soon as she came back to Dunfermline, watching her new happiness gratefully with wide, careful eyes, but saying nothing, as was his way.

Some weeks after her return, when the misty air of autumn was blue and still above the distant sea, she met him coming down the stairs from the queen's bower with a small satisfied smile on his face.

He stopped on the turn of the stairs.

"I have given the Queen my shell," he said.

"Your shell!" Merca stared at him, for he might as well have said he had given her his life. "Your *shell!*"

"Yes. She will keep it for me in her casket, with all her other treasures. I am grown now, and have no need of it."

Still his sister stared, and then he smiled his slow, sweet smile, and suddenly Merca smiled back. There on the cold stone staircase of the tower, they saw clearly in each other's eyes their future and their safety; both of them in the loved hands of Margaret, Queen of Scotia, and Malcolm, the King.

At the time *The Queen's Blessing* opens in 1070, William the Conqueror, from Normandy, had been ruling England for four years, but there were still many uprisings led by people who wished to restore a Saxon king to the throne. Malcolm supported the claim of Aedgar, and led a revolt which was to be supported by the Northumbrian Earl Gospatric, and by the Danish Fleet, who had among them a ship with Aedgar and his sisters, the Princesses Margaret and Christina, and their mother, Princess Agatha, on board. Malcolm's revolt failed because the Earl Gospatric turned traitor and went south to make peace with William, and the Danish Fleet sailed for home. Malcolm laid Northumbria to waste in his anger, but on reaching Wearmouth, he made arrangement to meet the ship carrying the Princess Margaret and her family.

Once before he had met the Princess Margaret in London, and on this second meeting he fell instantly in love with her. She and her family were now homeless, so he invited them to his Palace at Dunfermline, and there they made their way by sea, while he returned home with his army overland. Malcolm and Margaret were married within a few months in the little church in the Palace of Dunfermline.

The part of the story that concerns Merca and Dag is entirely imaginary—I have set them into a historical background that is as accurate as I can make it. All the facts about Queen Margaret come basically from the Life written by Father Turgot, who was one of the thirteen Benedictine Monks who followed her to settle in the monastery down the hill from the palace.

All the facts about Dunfermline tell of it as it was— a huddle of wattle buildings on the lip of a glen, until Queen Margaret laid her hand on it, and turned it into the most splendid court in the British Isles.

She was a most beautiful and remarkable lady, who had great influence on the people of Scotland. She was charming and gay and always most splendidly dressed, yet so holy and good that after her death, she was made a saint.

WATTLE

A method of building used at this time, where pliant reeds were woven through wooden uprights to make a wall. This was then covered with wet mud, and in better class dwellings, plastered over on the inside.

THEGNS AND JARLS

These were noblemen of the period, when the language was still much influenced by the Vikings. A "Jarl" was the Viking word that became the English "Earl."

OFFICE

This is the singing of the day's prayer by monks at certain prescribed times throughout the twenty-four hours.

AETHELING

This was the second name of Margaret's brother Aedgar, and means in effect "the young."

From her earliest days in Ireland, Madeleine Polland had a passionate interest in words which was coupled with the same involvement with people, so it is not surprising that she began to create people herself—out of words.

After completing school in England, she planned to be a painter, but circumstances changed her decision. During World War II she served for four years with the WAAF and it was then that she first began to write— short plays and entertainments for her friends. After the war Mrs. Polland married, and a home and two children kept her occupied until 1960, when a friend suggested that she write a book. She did just that, and *Children of the Red King* was selected as an honor book in the New York *Herald Tribune* Spring Book Festival.

Since then she has written several books for children: *Beorn the Proud* was also a *Herald Tribune* honor book, and a third, *The Town Across the Water*, was chosen by the New York *Times* as one of the 100 Best Books of the Year. A dedicated interest in history has made the setting of the author's books authentic—Mrs. Polland was born in Ireland, but moved to England at an early age and has never ceased to explore the heritage of her countries.

Mrs. Polland's husband is with the University of London, and they live in London with their two children, Charlotte and Fergus. She finds time to write only during "term," when her husband is busy at the University, and her children are away at school. The Polland holidays are devoted entirely to "raising the roof."